Ambition's Progress Part 1

B. Mathew
Ambition's Progress Part 1
Fictional Poetic Allegory

PARTRIDGE
A Penguin Random House Company

To order additional copies of this book, contact
Toll Free 800 101 2657 (Singapore)
Toll Free 1 800 81 7340 (Malaysia)
orders.singapore@partridgepublishing.com

www.partridgepublishing.com/singapore

CONTENTS

ACKNOWLEDGEMENT

Special appreciation to my dear daughters, Janet Mathew & Esther Mathew for their tireless efforts in preparing this manuscript for print and publication.

Dedicated to my dear wife Sundari Mathew

I have written other books as well; Christian faith, prophetic & deliverance series, including legal writings. These recent writings were easy for me today. But for Ambition's Progress Part 1, it was no easy task for me. Today, I am unable to answer, how I wrote it, why I wrote, the reasons for writing in outdated language and so on.

I wrote Ambition's Progress Part 1 in the year 1981 at a time where there were no computers or Microsoft word, no advance dictionary, no internet, no access to good libraries. I did not have any academic papers in literature or philosophy. I did not have the comfort of a white-collar 8.00 am to 5.00 pm job. The only thing I had was my dear wife. She was my inspiration, my source of comfort & encouragement. As I wrote with my ink and pen on crude papers, she did the typing in an old type-writer of good-old days. Without mystic inspiration you cannot create poetic literature. As such, without her coming into my life, I could have never created Ambition's Progress Part 1

B Mathew
August 2010

Introduction by Pritpal Singh

AMBITION'S PROGRESS Part 1

by b mathew

The author's first literary work, and MASTERPIECE, written in 1981.

This fictional work is an Allegory written in flowery classical English of prose and verse.

It has abundant allusions, bringing to life and excitement the beauty of classical mythology, western legends, Biblical stories, literature and poetry.

This archaic writing of an allegory set in poetical verses may not fit contemporary literature.

But for those who enjoy works by Shakespeare, John Milton or Bunyan this work will certainly be cherished.

A treasure and a marvelous discovery lay hidden and buried in the entire plot, story, verses and allusions in **Ambition's Progress Part 1**.

I count it a great pleasure to not only write this introductory note but to also have the honour to encourage my good friend to take the first step in printing and publishing this great literary work;

B MATHEW writes an allegory in the year 1981, called
AMBITION'S PROGRESS PART 1.

But unfortunately, my good friend had this great work buried and kept dead since its completion in 1983. It was through a casual conversation a passing remark was made by my friend of a literary work he had once written but was never published. I then took the opportunity to persuade him to have it printed and published.

This book is a fiction story. But this book is also poetry. And this book is also a philosophy on principles of success. You can read it like a novel or fairytale story. You can also read it like poetry or philosophy.

This allegory is written in classical English language with verses in poetry and allusions. The plot of this fairytale allegory is about a vagabond called Mr. Ambition, who lives in the City of Penury. This city of Penury is ruled by a horrible monster called Lord Poverty. In this city of Penury, this vagabond suffers great disgrace & reproach. One day, a good man by the name of Mr. Think Rich meets Mr. Ambition and encourages him to run away from the city of Penury and escape to another city called the City of Prosperity.

But however, the long journey to that City of Prosperity is filled with great and terrible dangers and deadly snares, where there are many giants, monsters and demons and unimaginable deadly traps. As such, advises Mr. Think Rich, that Mr. Ambition must first make a detour to a mystical labyrinth called the Garden of Sorrow to seek out a mysterious giant called Mr. Other-Self. Because only Mr. Other-Self could safely guide Mr. Ambition to the city of Prosperity.

At the entrance of the mystical Garden of Sorrow, Mr. Ambition meets Mr. Destiny. Mr. Destiny thereafter knights him as Sir Ambition the gallant Argonaut. But however, Sir Ambition finds himself overwhelmed by great misfortunes inside the garden of Sorrow. Where following a terrible battle with the horrible giant called Suicide, Sir Ambition is captured by the monster, Unemployment and imprisoned in a labour camp called, Hard-Manual-Labour Estate. Here the monster Unemployment maims Sir Ambition by digging out one of his eyes. But with the aid of an alter-ego, Sir Auto-Suggestion, Sir Ambition escapes Hard-Manual-Labour estate, but with Unemployment on hot pursued. In Sir Ambition's search for the mysterious man, Other-Self, he accidently stumbles upon a mysterious kingdom called, the Kingdom of Within.

Here he is welcomed and nursed. After his wounds are healed, the king of this Kingdom of Within and his valiant gladiators escort Ambition out in his search for the elusive Mr. Other-Self.

Then once again, the grisly monster, Unemployment confronts Ambition, the valiant king and knights from the kingdom of Within. But the monster, Unemployment easily overpowers and destroys these valiant men and fatally wounds Ambition, leaving him to die a painful and slow death. But with the help of his alter-ego and others, Ambition gathers his feeble strength and continue searching for the mysterious man, Mr. Other-Self.

Finally Ambition stumbles upon a strange glittering Kingdom of GreatWithin and makes a last and final attempt to awaken the mysterious man, Other-Self. Sir Ambition succeeds in setting into motion the awakening process but soon dies from his fatal wounds.

But even though Ambition dies, he dies with anticipated hope of a resurrection from death, knowing that Mr. Other-Self shall raise him up. Part 1 ends with the awakening process of the invincible man Other-Self.

Preface

I had recently looked up my old cabinet in search of a certain Christian devotional book when I saw an old worn out almost decayed file. I took it out curiously, dust it out and to my surprise it was an old, old type written manuscript, almost worn out, almost moth eaten and faded but still intact.

Only then did I realize it was something I had written or more correctly something I had created 30 years ago, but had totally forgotten and discarded. Now I wondered how I wrote!

30 years ago back in 1981, a month following my blissful marriage to my dear wife, I commenced writing a literary work in between my busy working hours where I was working 12 to 16 hours a day in the factory as manual worker, where rarely do I get a rest day.

My wife did all the typing in an old antique type-writer of good old days. When my first daughter Janet was born in 1983, almost half of it was done and before my eldest daughter's first birthday cake cutting my wife completed typing out the whole manuscript of Ambition's Progress Part 1.

And 30 years later that is in 2010 after the aforementioned retrieval of this old worn out manuscript I asked my second daughter Esther to reproduce it in Microsoft word document for printing. I decided that I will not in any way tamper or change nor amend the original text of this fictional allegory set in poetic style riddled by abundant allusion, save and except where graphic images appear to elucidate the allusions.

This work may not appeal to the man in omnibus as would a novel or fictional writings. But for those who are conversant in English literature and in particular works by Shakespeare, Milton, Bunyan or Homer would certainly be enriched by Ambition's Progress Part 1

B MATHEW Author—July 2010

Forward by Author—May 1983

This fictional work is an Allegory written in both modern English and flowery classical English of prose and verse respectively. It has abundant allusions, bringing to life and excitement the beauty of classical mythology, western legends, Biblical stories, literature and poetry.

This fictional allegory is about a man called Sir Ambition making an extreme perilous journey from the city of Penury to the city of Prosperity. A dangerous journey where he needs to battle horrible giants, monsters and demons. A journey fraught with perilous snares.

Sir Ambition receives advice to first make a detour to a mystical Garden enroute his destination to seek out and invoke the aid of a mysterious sleeping giant called Mr. Other-Self. Because, only Mr. Other-Self could safely conduct and guide Sir Ambition to the city of Prosperity.

Part 1, focuses on Sir Ambition's dangerous venture into the mystical Garden and his macabre struggles inside this Garden. And towards the end of Part 1, Sir Ambition is unfortunately crushed by Misfortune and is mortally wounded. But just before Sir Ambition dies, he accidently awakens the mysterious sleeping giant, Mr. Other-Self. This awakening of Mr. Other-Self brings about misfortune to Misfortune itself when Mr. Other-Self by his mysterious powers resurrects and brings back to life the dead Sir Ambition. Part 1 ends here.

This work may not appeal to a common man as archaic writings of allegory may be out of today's fashion. But for those who enjoy works by Shakespeare, John Milton or Bunyan this work will certainly be cherished.

Should any erudite masters of English literature might find this work grossly in want of expected benchmarks of literary standards, for example, interalia verses contained herein may fall short of iambic pentameter of blank verses, then their justified indignation and qualified criticism would most certainly be allayed if given to their understanding that the writer is merely a below average and unread factory labourer who is not a product of any higher institution of learning and therefore not worthy to unlace the shoes of these grand masters or even the most feeble student of English literature. As such and therefore, for all who would endeavour a reading of this work but who would dismiss it on account of its grand verbosity, archaic language, and mystical allusions should bear in mind the author's infirmity as pleaded.

For those who would assail the author of adopting elements from past literary Giants, the author wishes to plead that if Isaac Newton himself is permitted to stand on shoulders of predecessor giants then why not the author. Furthermore, is an allegory an exclusive property of Bunyan, or are blank verses and poetry exclusive properties of Shakespeare and Milton?

For those who would give their strongest disapproval of writing an allegory in archaic language and outdated style, the author wishes to plead, doth not treasures of ages past and buried in historical deeps uncovered, appreciated and displayed proudly by contemporary argonauts of archeology in very present times.

Then again the critics may ask why then are the dialogue verses strewn in riddles of allusions and hard to understand metaphors and conversation of characters taking a bizarre detour to legends and apparent unrelated geographical places when such dialogues could be direct, clear and simple? For example, when Mr. Diffidence queries Sir Ambition as to why the need to seek the mysterious man Mr. Other-Self, Sir Ambition in answering Mr. Diffidence takes a detour as follows;

For by him shall my nights be inflamed with lights,
As like those flicking lights on hillocks at the foot
Of the Big Hill in Aurea Chersonese during the Fiesta
Of the La Bon Lady, Sainte Anne . . .

Here Sir Ambition while answering Mr. Diffidence's question takes a bizarre detour to the night images and candle-light scenes of the saint Ann's feast held at Bukit Mertajam, Malaysia, where the whole hill is lighted up with candle lights by masses of St. Ann devotees thronging by hundreds of thousands, a breath taking scene viewed from afar at night. Ambition through this allusion conveys to Diffidence that his misfortunes would all come to an end when he finds Mr. Other-Self and new light of hope would spring forth thereafter. And in the succeeding verses, Sir Ambition takes even a deeper and further detour to tell Diffidence that thus far and hitherto everyone including divine providence has failed to help him and his last and only hope is in finding Mr. Other-Self.

As such, in answering why such allusions to riddles of myths, legendary sites, memorial locations and metaphors, the author avers the axiom that the invisible elements are more real than the visible, the hidden more real than the unhidden, the sub-conscious greater than the conscious. A great, mystical, mysterious, immortal, glorious message and truth and revelation and treasure and a marvelous discovery lay hidden and buried in the entire plot, story, verses and allusions in Ambition's Progress Part 1. That in years and epochs to come a never ending endeavour of continuous and fresh discovery of rich treasures await in this literary work of

'THE AMBITION'S PROGRESSPART I.'

WHAT'S THIS WORK ALL ABOUT"

- The essence of this fictional work is the allegorization of a struggle against poverty, dramatizing the mysteries of life and suffering, the inner conflicts between positive and negative faces (emotions) in a man and his mystical link with divinity written under the similitude of a dream.

THE PLOT:

- The story is about the progress (journey) of a vagabond and the protagonist named Sir Ambition, escaping his abhorred homeland called, the city of Penury to another elysian land called, the city of Prosperity; an odyssey fraught with perils.

- **Part one**
  Portrays his venture and travailing agonies at a mystical Labyrinth called the Garden of Sorrow, climaxing in his accidental discovery of a strange kingdom and the awakening of a mysterious sleeping giant, while part two would portray his actual journey to the city of prosperity. (I intend to work on part II only after the publication of part I) Both parts contain his battles against formidable giants and fiends and he encounters characters like Mr. Think Rich, Sir Hope, Mr. Auto-suggestion, Mr. Fatalist, Dr. Time and many others.

THE SUMMARY:

The story begins as a dream, with the writer falling "into a deep deep slumber and behold I dreamed a strange dream." He sees a wretched vagabond named Ambition in a strange dirty city called the city of Penury being abused, scorned and persecuted by fellow citizens and his own family. At such a deplorable state, the ostracized man meets a wonderful man, Mr. Think Rich from another city, who then directs him to another land so as to free himself from all miseries. But the odyssey, Mr. Think Rich warns, is fraught with perils and abominable titans and hence Ambition has to enter a mystical labyrinth by way of his destination called the Garden of Sorrow. He has to enter this mystical Garden to seek out a mysterious man named Mr. Other-self who alone could protect and conduct him safely through all the dread perils to the city of Prosperity.

But the protagonist finds himself stormbound at the metaphysical Garden; where following a terrible battle with the grisly giant, Suicide, at the valley of Broken-Heartedness he is captured by a heinous titan called Unemployment. He is also persecuted and made to toil at a labour camp called, Hard Manual Labour Estate before making his escape through the help of Mr. Auto—Suggestion to discover two strange kingdoms. After which he gets in touch with that mysterious man, Mr. Other-Self, who is also called the sleeping giant. Part I ends here.

THE STYLE

- The narrations and descriptions are in modern English whereas the dialogues, soliloquies and poems are written in classical English. Fused together with the dialogues in blank-verse are copious allusions and stories from Greek and Roman mythology, the Bible, classical philosophy, theology, legends, geography etc. To dramatize mysteries of realities, inner antagonism and the metaphysical link with divinity I resorted to an elaborate style of using allusions. Apart from this the allusions also serve to embellish the blank—verse.

You are now about to STEP into a Dreamland World

of an Allegory,

AMBITION'S PROGRESS PART 1

where ancient legends, mythological heroes, poetic

wisdom & Biblical stories are about to become alive

and they await to greet you

The Fairy Tale Allegory unfolds in the next page

AMBITION'S PROGRESS PART 1
(commenced writing on December 1981)

Chapter 1

In the City of Penury

In the throes of a chronic unemployment, as the saturnine clouds of depression and despair hovered over me, while being forced to stand thunderstruck and watch the social predicament I was in; my life being at a brink of an object ruin with no hope of regaining a place in the world, I had to face another wonton plight of an inward disorientation, that was the disintegration of my confidence and personal look.

All of my pathetic and ardent attempts to embark upon a career were futile.

The sight of friends and people with secure and senior positions coerced me into a dungeon of inferiority and remorse. Interview after interviews failed.

Prayer after prayer failed. Not a scintilla of human source or aid I could have recourse to.

Amidst the dreaded howling of fear and hopelessness I travelled miles to see a job, only to be slapped by another disappointment, an affront more than this mortal soul could take.

Brutally stabbed in the already mauled heart by another cruel knife of failure, grasping for the ebbing breath of life and floundering to hold back the blood of sanity, I staggered pass in macabre agony the busy street decked with glittering lights and arrogantly display goods of the city's complexes and yawing to a lonely park lane I fell upon one of the arbour's bench to placate the effeteness of my body and spirit.

I soon felt into a deep, deep, slumber.

And behold, I dreamt a strange dream.

Lo, I beheld a disheveled wretched man clothed in dirty, torn rags dragging his emaciated body slowly; his unshaven cadaverous countenance shriveled with discouragement, hopelessness and sulked eyes glaringly implied that he was an ostracized derelict.

As he walked pass the crowded street with a stick on one hand and a dirty bundle hung by his back, the slum dwellers mocked, some laughed, hurled abusive words while others spat on him.

But he was oblivious to these rains of scorn and seemed to be wrapped with some great burden of his mind.

Now this strange place was strewn all over with rotting waste and shabby huts and I perceived that it was called the City of Penury.

Suddenly, a loud noise shrieked through the welkin like that of a thunder.

And to my horror I beheld a fiend-looking being, thundering forth upon a pale horse towards this wretched man.

As it came galloping, upheaveling whirlwind of dust and dirt behind, the people with one accord shouted:

"Hail **Lord DEBT**, who cometh in the name of His Highness the king of Penury!"

The creature was hideous to behold; loomed as a Cyclop, with a scorpion tail-like horn protracting from its forehead, fumes of fire belching out from its dragonish mouth and nose and a bulk hirsute body with a serpent-like tail.

As Lord Debt came racing, wielding its penal whip, the people fell prone to the ground in veneration with the exception of the ragamuffin who stood defying.

As the beast pulled its enormous horse to a mighty halt, the wretched man suddenly looked up as if he had perceived an impending infernal torture.

He stood petrified as pangs of fear seized him.
The vicious gorgon's eye was now fixed upon him and in a stentorian bellow it thus spoke:

"Thou fool! I abhor thy very sight. Thou art a disgrace to his majesty's name, the Almighty Lord Poverty!"

But before the poor man could absorb the rebuke, the beast leapt from its horse to set upon him.

As the hideous monster vented its rage one could conceive the brutal torture as a horrendous catastrophe. For it whipped and kicked the poor man about.

The poor man wailed, pleaded for mercy and writhed about the bloody ground like a bruised worm, while the people gathered to muse over the torture.

After this Lord Dept leapt on to its horse and rode off as swiftly as it had appeared.

The man hauling his bruised body out of the bloody mud and staggered towards his home, only to greet teeming scorn from his family.

Drifting then to the nearby woods, finding a cool mountain stream, he sat by a stone, and there burying his face on to his hands he wept aloud.

As he wailed, I saw a man with a refulgent countenance and in white apparel coming towards him.

His name was Mr. Think Rich:

Think Rich: O wretched man! Wherefore draineth thou dry,
                The Lamenting waters of dark **Cocytus!**
                What be the reason for such great wailings,
                That would not be comforted?

Wretched Man: O Sir, the bowels of mine woeful soul,
                Is a desolate **Death Valley**.
                Behold, an ostracized plebeian am I,
                Whose bread and wine is but scorn and
                persecution,
                With a dainty meat of stark misery.
                My neighbours and friends hold me now in such
                bitter Derision,
                By reason of mine Imprisonment which I suffered
                of late.

Think Rich: Say'st thou imprisonment!
                By what hideous crime or was it transgression of
                statute,
                Or it was by thine own wonton sowing of nettle
                seeds,
                That thou shouldest incur the ire of thine people,
                And become worthy of this deplorable plight,
                And reap its kind?

Wretched Man: Yea Sir Yea, a crime and evil transgression,
                And also wonton sowing:
                To enlighten thee in this matter,
                Must I needs to take thee thitherward of mine life's
                gloomy lane.

Once was mine sojourn hither honourable,
And respected by neighbours and family,
Till met I a very remarkable man called, Mr. Aim-High.
And the mutual yearn to forthwith set us both at liberty,
From the swadling maukin of mediocrity,
Did compel us to enter upon such a business league,
That was in defiance of our kingdom's statute.
Betwixt us thence, many a privy conferences were held,
To prosper an ideal and crafty plan;
For sought we surreptitiously together to leave our city,
And to sow and reap anew at a nearby town called, Venture.
But alas, in the midst of our great plans,
We were foiled and deflowered by law's eye.
Wherefore our strong king, his highness
Lord Poverty had poor Mr. Aim-High cruelly executed,
And me beaten up and imprisoned.
Sith then and hitherto the seamy nymphs had wax mine myrmidons,
While Demogorgon diverted the course of Acheron thro' mine stable.

Think Rich: Sith then, hath not the iris arch appeared
              upon thine saturnine cloud?
              Wherefore remain'st thou upon the mire?

Wretched Man: Behold Sir, the vines in portly clusters, thriving
              resplendently upon the land of Canaan,
              And the cereals that ov'r floweth the oriental barns,
              Are ever comforted, by the loving Pact of the Iris Arch.
              The scourged bones, upon that open Champaign,
              Hath their hope in the breath of the Logos.
              The Gibeonites in their sore plight wielded
              their craft to wrest out alms of mercy from the
              Everlasting Arm, which once led the Chosen Seed
              thro' Central Palestine.

But what hope hast this forlorn destitute man?
For hope that visiteth all, keepeth not an Obolus,
for an errand to the shades.
Prometheus did receive his sound reprieve, when
the Greater Light slumbereth beneath the horizon;
But not this cursed cipher.
Nor do I possess the strength to survive the ireful deluge,
As like in fable once, mighty Deucalion and sweet
Pyrrha,
Who 'scaped judgment in the age of iron.
For He who bindeth and no wight ev'r could'st unbind,
And who sealeth and no man could'st unseal,
Yea for He hath cruelly chained me to the dank
craggy fires of Tartarus!
Hoist thy ears Sir! 'Tis like to be fettered to the
Needles of Wight amidst a tempest,
With mad Chaos and adamantine Nox to perform
their macabre dance around!
Alas! Hope is beyond mine Ken,
And, weltering alone mine den.

Think Rich: What haply, if I throw the pearl that shall provide
                 the open sesame to thy deliverance,
                 Will it be a worthy cast?

Wretched Man: Sir! I swear 'twill nev'r be cast upon swines!
                 Hitherto have I chastened my knees, wet the hard
                 priedieu and received but forlorn answers.
                 Sir, kindness and hope is graven upon thine
                 countenance as of the sacred **Decalog upon that
                 table by Oreb.**
                 Me seems thou art like that **good man, Help,
                 who lifted Christian of old** out of the Slough of
                 Despond.

Think Rich: But son, an empty hand wooeth not a Hawk.

Wretched Man: Make known then the price required of me.

B Mathew

Think Rich: Harken unto me! 'Tis the price of an odyssey,
                yea, transcending all that thou hast ever heard or
                known before,
                For lieth there a great land far beyond;
                'Tis called, the city of Prosperity.
                Hark, the day thou makest upon the stronds
                of this Land, then shall thy captivity turn back and
                thine enemies shall bow in shame before thee,
                While the tormentors themselves shall be tormented.
                At this Beulah Land are several villages, wherein thou
                could'st make thy tranquil sojourn in full freedom;
                Some of their names are Fulfillment, Sound-Mind,
                Further knowledge and Riches.

Wretched Man: Pray Sir, wherefore tormenteth thou a starving man!
                Hasten to set my foot thither!

Think Rich: Come away then O wretched man.

   He then led him deeper into the woods:

Think Rich: What 's thy name?

Wretched Man: Ambition, is my name Sir,
                Though wretched am I without, yet in the nethermost
                region of mine forlorn being, there lieth still a glowing
                coal, a worm that dieth not.

Think Rich: We've arrived! Yon is the way, and must thou begin
                thither.
                Hark to the letters Son,
                Wilt thou be freed from the fetters of scorn, remorse,
                persecution, turmoil, misery, want and destitution?

Ambition: Yea Sir yea!
                More than Sisyphus seekest reprieve,
                O, much more than the issues of **Uranus and
                Gaia** would strive to break asunder the bars of the

nethermost gaol!

Yea hark, much more than a doe lost upon the Algerian weary land seekest water.

Prithee Sir, before I betake myself to this odyssey, wilt thou not breakforth some profitable instructions,

Whereby I could graven it upon mine heart and mind.

Think Rich: Hark then, thy odyssey is plenished in fulsome with snares, formidable titans, perils, **monsters and demons.**

In fact, thou hast to battle thy way thro' the dreaded Pandemonium itself to get thee yon City of Prosperity.

Therefore gird up thy loins, to withstand such horrendous pograms,

This shall redound to thine first water.

Ambition: By betaking such progress will I not be ensnared betwixt clashing Bosporus,

If mine mortal strength were to betray me?

How then Sir? For me-seems thine pragmatism hast no savour.

Think Rich: Fear not, I wot all thine apprehensions;

The incorruptible victuals do I have.

When thou betakest upon thy progress from hither,

Thou shalt anon within short space come upon a mystical place, called Garden of Sorrow.

Therein dwelleth a mysterious but a wonderful man, named Mr. Other-Self.

Let thine study be to seek him,

For he shall conduct thee safely thro' every perils and snares unto the City of Prosperity.

Now, hoist thine ears to the very letter;

Thou should'st in nowise leave Sorrow's Garden, to continue thy progress without Mr. Other-Self.

Ambition: Sir, thou didst mention about giants and demons,

How then could I battle them?
Will they not devour me in their ferociousness as
Crones his issues?

Think Rich: Now let not thine heart swoon because of such
titanic villains.
If thou goest under the aegis of Mr. Other-Self,
Then, would it become of the titans of what
became beyond the bourns of great Moab by Ar, of
Zamzummims.

Ambition: But Sir, heretofore have I not beheld or known that
mystical garden.
And where, and how am I to seek that mysterious man?

Think Rich: Trust me, if thine purpose and perseverance playeth
no infidelity, then will he be surely found of thee.
Nevertheless, must I now acquaint thee with thine
victuals.
(Takes out a golden ring)
Marvel not, this is a magical ring,
Whose wonders outshineth ev'n the combined
virtues of Astolpho's horn and book.
When thou throw'st this golden ring upon the
ground, a gladiator will appear to serve thee,
Whose name is Mr. Auto-Suggestion.
Should'st thou no longer need him, then, at thine
behest, he shall return to his formal form.
This is the golden ring. Here, wear it!
(Gives him the golden ring and takes out a
silver ring)

Do likewise also with this silver ring,
For it is thy panoply to arm thee from tip of thy head
to the very sole of thy feet. (Gives him)

Ambition: Behold how mine heart aches for joy!
Yea striking it asunder will a goddess of thanksgiving

spring forth to adore thee Sir For eternity.
In truth I wot not how to thank thee.

Think Rich: My reward of eternal joy is upon thine deliverance.
From hence forth art thou no longer a wretched man.
Thou art now an argonaut!
I now bid thee Godspeed.
Go thine way! Aureole!

Night supplanted by the Hamera of hope, hauling him out of the tormenting labyrinth of despond and face scintillating with confidence, he took upon the odyssey at once and headed off rejoicing, to a land far beyond called city of Prosperity which shall ultimately obliterate all his woes.

As he went, he espied a man running towards him. His name was Mr. Feeble-Will and Ambition accosted him:

Ambition: O my friend, wherefore the need for such haste!
Thy whey-face conveyeth omen. What . . .

Feeble.-Will: You Sir, whither away in this light manner?
That durst deem thy life so lightly!

Ambition: As I am informed by a good man, I should make unto the Garden of Sorrow, before I proceed further on my long progress to the City of Prosperity.

Feeble.Will: Get you back Sir with haste, nay, append wings to thy flight!
O Sir! Thou walk'st blindly into **a deadly Minotaur's** labyrinth!
Not a Theseus to deliver thy life,
Hark, nor a silken twined ball to back-track,
Wherefore Sir, heed mine words, return forthwith!

Ambition: Friend haply thy fears are without any foundation.
               Enlighten me further as to what or whom thou
               saw'st or heard.

Feeble-Will: I canst not linger any further Sir.
               My fears are, even now the triad sisters may be
               eavesdropping on our exchanges.
               Wherefore I beg thine leave!

With this Mr. Feeble-Will fled leaving the argonaut stunned in a quandary.

Chapter 2

Gates of Garden of Sorrow

But nonetheless, he continued till be reached the entrance gate to the Garden of Sorrow. Standing by the gate was a porter named Destiny:

Ambition: Good day Sir, I am come from the city of Penury and bound for that city of Prosperity.
Wherefore must I needs to past this gate, unto the mystical Garden.

Destiny: My good friend, in buxomnesse to whose voice, hast thou taken this odyssey?

Ambition: A wonderful man called Mr. Think Rich.

Destiny: Friend, hast he not told thee of the perils?

Ambition: Yea Sir!

Destiny: And by this, perceive I that the big horn of foison hath made thine eyes myopic to the sword of Damocles which hangeth ov'r the Garden of Sorrow.
Many valiants, yea greater than thou hath ventured upon this garden, alas, to their ignominious Bane.
For the mystic Garden of Sorrow is a labyrinth,
Lurked therein are Titans, Demons, snares and all

manner of perils.

A tide ago there was one man called Feeble-Will hither, aspiring to venture,

And would not yield unto mine entreaties to turn back.

But when a strange bellow shrieked, he fled for his life.

Ambition: Hark Sir, whether I be blind or forlore in swevenes, I truly wist not.

But then, of this am I so sure;

The die is cast and yond side of Rubicon have I reached.

Wherefore I now do receive thy warnings with outstretched cavalier arms!

Sir, thy words did make their good hit, but then mine wax sealed obsession refuseth to unbind me,

That I might incline unto thine red heeds.

Destiny: In the intensity of thine obsession hast thou connived at the trouble-waters of the deep!

Amidst a petrifying tryst with the deep's white tiger wilt thou then seek to turn, but t'will be past hope to battle ashore.

Thou art blind to the dark mysteries,

Herein, darker than that of **Hecate,**

The mother and queen of dread sorcery.

Thy presumptuous aura limneth the nature of an ostrich, which is found sore wanting in wisdom,

For it regardeth nor careth for her young ones.

Thou lovest nor carest for thy life by exposing it to perils.

Prithee, make from a certain bane.

Ambition: Prithee Sir, garrotte not the inner man with such garished, baseless admonishing.

For to an argonaut, fears are chimeras.

Doth a seemingly frail squid cower at the sight of the deep's ferocious tiger?

Tho' weak, yet wielding its ink it turneth the beast

back.
Likewise hath the grief smitten Man not halted short
of what he spake of an ostrich, thou would'st have
learnt this great truth;
Draw nigh a brooding mother, and thou would'st
taste its forked shaft claws,
For in such fury and passion she guard'st her little
ones.
Nor doth my defense nor mine victuals breakforth
unto thine perception;
'Tis hidden like an ink of a squid or octopus.
Therefore fear not for mine life, I'll fare well,
Even now Sir, the **Elysian Plains of joy,**
Beckons me to come yonder for reprieve;
('Tis like those woeful souls crying out yon
when ferried down the dank hateful river)
How could I be still and harden mine heart!
Nay! Come what may, I shall outface all storms.
Nor shall the Good Adonai forsake me;
For He shall surely harken, heed mine calls,
Yea, just as like once when that Mortal Heel,
In the turmoil of his spleen stood all alone,
By a lonely strond one lorn night by Troy,
While those bliss romantic waves were making their
amorous dashes against stubborn rocks,
Cried aloud to his immortal mother,
Who hearing his frantic cries hastened then unto
his aid.

Destiny: Harken unto this;

T'was a prodigy to brag, alas a folly that slew pardon.
All paternal pleas to revoke his boon could not be taken.
But binding up regretful Apollo with Styx's strong cord,
He vaulted grinning upon the smiling chariot to abode,

Gathering those fearful and fateful rein with his virgin hands,

For that supercilious arrogance he possessed had no ends.
Beckoning Rosy Slender Beauty to open Drowsy Morn gate,
He took upon that deadly pegasean errand of sad fate.
And the harvest of his folly;
Sought the terrified stars and moon refuge, from that leashing storms,
Tell me, how could these poor fellows withstand those fiery pelting bombs,
T'was a day when Founts and Rivers went begging for watery alms,
Arose that sardonic Black-Sea to show his grimacing thumbs,
And to felicitate the wights of Africa and India,
A folly that awoke the enraged god who at Olympus has no peer,
Greenish Faun together with Pan fled the ghost of cold,
O the folly that made Clotho's spinning jenny go so bold,
And which quickened, threw so very wild Lachesis's cruel torsion,
While happy Atropos whetted her shear to teach a lesson,
Zeus beholding him screamed in wrath and vented in hideous puffs,
Wanting a lesson to teach he drew out the bellowing shafts;
Fell he O fell he bleeding and lost all life's property,
Clymene's propiatory crying gave her no lost propinquity,
The bereaved Heliades, those lovely limpid watery lasses,
Began grief-worn and forlorn to wash white their body-glasses,
By Eridanus, ceased not, whose sorrowful tears fall till this day,
But for this arrogant swain t'was a rich and rewarding pay.

Bethink O callow argonaut;
Thy life and thy loved ones, wilt thou have them all grieved, if woe betide thee?
Prithee my dear friend, make from perdition, beguile not thyself,
Hark, even the highest durst not venture against those storied titans without the Aegis.
When Earth, out of her rancor begot dread Typhon, the belching furnace,
Cowered the royal pair behind a ram and a kine.
Esteem not lowly the might of thine adversary.
'Tis nev'r delectable to grovel beneath oppressive tempest.

Answered Ambition: T'was by reason of a mother's turbid fears,
She hid the flame by a veil of feminine,

That she might save herself from bereavement tears,

And that he might not by Fame and Name be seen,

Nestled he amongst those mediocrity lasses,
Before the hearth of comfort and long life,

Came to meet, an obsession name Odysseus,

Tho' he would have a brief course with so much strife,

Yet across the horizons of time shall spread his fame.
By great venture, he built at last a great name.

Wherefore, I've cast my lot for fame and name.
Thou hath uttered amiss of mine loved ones and neighbours;
Tho' I be sent black berrying,
Venting such bristling pleas by the hand of Fate,
Yet not a ear, nor a kind heart could I expect or lean upon.
Hark Sir, they've reckoned mine indigence a felony.
But of this be thou assured; my wisdom shall never be burnished by vanity.
Cognizant am I of mine weaknesses,
And the formidable games that attend.
Wherefore Sir, mine study will be to seek a mighty mysterious man,
He is called—Mr. Other-Self; thus by his aegis
Will I proceed further from yon Garden.
Pray you Sir, wot thou who and what is he and whither be his sojourn?

Destiny: What! Say'st thou that mysterious man?

Ambition: Yea Sir yea!

Destiny: Friend, is thine compos mentis disarrayed!
                Seeking him, 'twill be like **Sisyphus floundering to
                get aloft that huge boulder!**
                In truth, no one wot who that strange man is, or
                whither be his stay in the Garden.
                And, many men hath perished while seeking him, in
                this Death favoured place:
                But I do know something about his great shocking
                powers!

Ambition: What be his powers Sir?

Destiny: Friend, his powers are terrible and might so horrible!
                No wretch can be the same after confronting him.
                Yea no powers, not even **Pluto**'s army could
                withstand nor prevail against him!
                My friend, even the dead, and the sapless can be
                raised!
                For such and many more untold wonders which
                mind durst not venture,
                Are the powers of that mysterious man, the Invincible
                Mr. Other-Self!
                Fortunate is the soul that is found of him!

Ambition: As thou bewrayed the iceburg tip wonders of him,
                began it to sear mine heart as it seared their hearts
                by **the road to Emmaus!**
                Upon mine very life vouch I, that I might plunge greater
                depth of his wonders and mysterious powers.
                Thy fueling word hath lighted a fiery flaming love for
                him.
                Now Sir, prithee yield thy gates.

Destiny: Friend, bethink! Let not thine head boil over!
                'Tis a Sisyphean task to seek him!

Ambition: Pray you sir, without much ado make from the Juggernaut!

Try not with it!

Destiny: At last, thou hast made thine tryst with destiny!

I shall fling wide the gates for you.

But hark, before thou venture forth, must I need to knight thee.

Come to thine knees!

(Ambition kneels before him, and Destiny placing a sword upon his head then)

I now knight thee O man! Henceforth thou art called and named Sir Ambition! the argonaut!

Arise! O Argonaut! (opens the gate)

Behold now, Sir Ambition, three pathways that diverge,

Tho' they be thus so, yet shall they converge at the Garden.

Their names areTragedy, Lost of Love and Health Failure.

Thou may'st choose any one of these paths.

Now, go thy way, Sir Ambition!

Chapter 3

Sir Ambition's First Tragedy

His assiduous demeanour paved way for his objective, he went forth, in discretion pondered still for some time and then chose the second pathway leading to that arcane Garden.

In my dream a strange premonitory voice warned that he must be heading towards a simmering ground where portentous fiends of terror, on diabolical prowl await him.

Now, he had not as yet headed far when the pathway seemed to close in and on either side grew the lush green woods denser.

The awaking darkness joined by the howling of wolves and goblins enchained his tensed heart with loneliness. Suddenly spotted he a white figure a far off heading towards him.

He stood still. Behold, a dazzling damsel with an endearing smile greeted him.

He stood speechless as the whirlwind of romance swooped him up to an empyrean ecstasy, fumigating his frazzled mind and spirit of all ennui.

The damsel's name was Romance Love.

The stunned argonaut then:

Ambition: O thou piercing damsel,
                Say, art thou come, at Cupid's behest?
                A devouring Harpy is thy sight!

Romance Love: Pray you Sir set at rest thine infected
                Argosy!
                I am come that thou may'st be decked with balm.
                Phoebus will anon retire his car,
                Wherefore let not thine feet to kair in this darkness,
                come away to mine home.

Ambition: What are you?

Romance Love: A lass of thine choice!

Ambition: What have you to do with me O strange lass?
                Quaint is thine voice that rings a Siren's song,
                Embarrass not mine purpose I prithee!

Romance Love: Prithee, limn not upon thine beholding a Calypso to
                embarrass,
                Yet in harmony to thy purpose have I come.
                Hast thou torn asunder with clairvoyance the great
                veil of infinite intelligence,
                To behold and comprehend the primordial plan and
                Purpose of Him from whom all blessings and virtues
                flow!

The poor man was taken aback by these words and followed her to a secluded bower enshrouded in a forest of flamboyant begonias and pine-trees.

I beheld in my dream the currents of change surging through the wretched man's life (for he was still in rags) so much so I wondered if she, Romance Love was that mysterious man whom Mr. Think Rich talk about; she began adorning him with a new clean face for his demurred countenance and a scintillating garment for his rags.

They then sat down to dine for the night:

Ambition: This man anew thou hast given amazes me!
           Wretched as I was hitherto in the sad confinement of loneliness,
           Till brought me you this emancipation proclamation.
           Meaning and purpose anew I behold such that I had n'ver seen.
           Even this scintillating appearance of mine seems so strange,
           The glass shall never grow weary.
           Mine fantasy thus;
           That this billow must never cease.

Romance Love: O argonaut, pray you, weary yourself not upon the glass,
           Lest shalt thou turn into a flowery Narcissus!

Ambition: A jasper art thou! Fear not, nev'r will I come upon such folly.
           Now, lest I forget, wot thou a strange mysterious man who liveth hither, whose name is Mr. Other-Self?
           I must needs to seek him out at all cost.

Romance Love: Nev'r have I heard of any such person or name.
           But nevertheless I have heard about a great SleepingGiant who is said, to be slumbering somewhere in a strange cave, calledWithin, just along the rough valley of Broken-Heartedness.
           But I wot not for certain.
           But wherefore labour'st thou in such visions?
           Hark, I can be thine all sufficiency,
           Cast off such visions, for I have in mind
           to crown thee with much delight.

They became enamored of each other: perhaps as a compensation for his plaintive past he enraptured himself in endless bacchanalian feast for several days and I conjectured that not a scintilla of his sacred objective was upon his mind.

In consternation I wondered if this juggernaut of romance might completely crush his purpose.

One morning they set out for Mt. Ecstasy a place decked with splendour and beauty, located right in the heart of this strange garden. Upon reaching its submit, in the delirium of their joy:

Ambition: **Mine life a seasons and mine soul a lands!**
Sweet damsel, all bitter seasons are turned
Pleasant! Mine weary thirsty land are ploughed
With milk and honey!

A Ballad on Seasons
Once upon a lovely dusky midnight,
Beheld mine happy eyes a ghastly sight,
Came by stealth a chilly harbinger
With purpose bad; ev'n to murder:
Kill   Kill   Kill
Stab Stab Stab
Kill ye Stab ye
Kill ye Stab ye
Hoisting his sword amidst the pyrrhic dance
Upon lively Vertumnus he did pounce;
Slaying him, off the stable slayer went.
Alas! the bleeding swains warm life laid spent:
Bled Bled Bled
Died Died Died
Bled he Died he
Bled he Died he
Mourning Flora rained her flowery showers
Juicy Pomona felt her rotting powers,
While ploughing Ops convulsed in dying pain,

Alas! life succombed to slumbering chain:
    Sleep, Sleep Sleep
    Ebb Ebb Ebb
    Sleep ye Ebb ye
    Sleep ye Ebb ye
Returned then the cruel slayer to reign
That hoary hail he did continually rain,
Desolate as Negeb the cauldron great,
Cry ye rustic youths! for cupid is dead;
    Cry Cry Cry
    Mourn Mourn Mourn
    Cry ye Mourn ye
    Cry ye Mourn ye
Broke the stygian shroud, ripped by heavenly car
Then soft rapturous songs were heard afar,
Slained Thazmuz jerked to life and sighed to sing,
At last! Rolled in the joy billows of spring.
    Roll Roll Roll
    Sing Sing Sing
    Roll ye Sing ye
    Roll ye Sing ye
Milky tufts in the joyful age of Gold,
Which that latter day seer proclaimed so bold,
Sprang forth within mine soul; for 'Tis summer!

For great is thine powers O Romantic Love!
It lifts, carry'st me thro', from the flowery showers of
Autumn to murderous winter,
To **rolling billows of spring,**
To throbbing Summer.
Mine weary soul rejuvenates with life **as Negeb** by
Edomites thrived.
Even the great father did find springs and food in
galore for his retinue in that Great Cauldron!
O I am anew, anew!

Romance Love: O argonaut, I'm eternal and can nev'r part from
thee, yea not ev'n death can have us part.

26

Perennial mine presence in all seasons;
For I am but, the lass of thine heart's choice,
Tho Death would us part, yet the memories of me
shall arise like the old Pheonix from its ash to
cherish and sustain thee thro' thy odyssey.
As the waves cease not upon the strands,
So will my memories pound upon thy heart.
Amid a rip-tide it will rent thee apart,
While in neap-tide t'will placate thy soul.
Even when thou betakes a sad stygian errand,
T'will draw nigh thee,
To show thee the seeds of genius.

Ambition: Now, wherefore speakest thou in this manner,
Casting me headlong from such profound joy?
Of departing, separation and death!
In truth say I unto thee, O mine lass,
If thou requitest not mine love, I'll wax surely then a
yellowery flower!

SONG

From the sheding of Aurora's tears,

To the boarding of the Golden Barque,

That languorous and lorn gaze which sears,

Even gods, yet a requital dark,

Languish O languish, O mine yellowery flower,

To win the rider of World-Candle thou'll never.

CHORUS

Tell me O tell me, O yellowery flower

Tell me O tell me, O yellowery flower

Those streamy mysteries of longing love

Those streamy mysteries of longing love

O mine lass, eternal will be mine love

for thee.

Romance Love: The hour cometh O argonaut! Arise!
I must now needs to recompense thee.

Her mien then grew demurred interjecting the gossamer ambience of romance while dark clouds, which formed a far off drifted towards them.

Yet the tipsy argonaut perceived not the ominous augury. She was quick to show him that cave—Within and a strange hill called Idea in the valley of Broken-Heartedness.

Poignantly taking out a garnet from her bosom:

Romance Love: Argonaut take this garnet, guard it well!
By this shalt thou find thine life.

With this she disappeared amidst the engulfing dark clouds. And it hit and crushed him like a gargantuan boulder; while the fantasy castle of living happily ever after came crumbling down to a shambles, he found himself hustled away into a midst of a turbulent ocean of loneliness.

Not being able to withstand the malevolent on-slaughter he fell into oblivion, slipped and fell tumbling down the slope of Mt. Ecstasy into the rugged valley of Broken-Heartedness.

After being washed ashore to his consciousness he picked himself up and wept bitterly. As he wept over his great loss an old man in white apparel and hoary beard approached him. His name was Compensation.

Compensation: Weep not O Argonaut!

Ambition: O Sir! How could'st I hold back this fountain,
              Aft tragedy hath performed its macabre dance?

Compensation: Son, hearken . . .

Ambition: Hearken? Nay, nay, Sir, the harsh reversals I had
              suffered are more than tongue can tell.
              O mine mangled and worked life seeks quietus in
              the blissful hands of Death.

Compensation: My Son, incline thine heart to these truths; The
              change which break up at short intervals the
              prosperity of men are advertisement of a nature
              whose law is growth. Evermore it is the order of
              nature to grow, and every soul is by this intrinsic
              necessity quitting its whole system of things, its
              friend and home, and laws, and faith, as the shellfish
              crawls out of its beautiful but stony case, because
              it no longer admits of its growth, and slowly forms a
              new house. And yet the compensations of calamity
              are made apparent to the understanding also after
              long intervals of time!

Ambition: Why should I suffer a love tragedy?

Compensation: Didst thou not choose the route of Lost of Love?
              Thou art the captain of thine destiny and the master
              of thine fate!

Ambition: But perceive not I the Compensation!

Compensation: A fever, a mutilation, a cruel disappointment, a loss of wealth, a loss of friends seems at the moment unpaid loss and unpayable. But the sure years reveal the deep remedial force that underlies all facts.

Ambition: Sir, what may be the compensations?

Compensation: The death of a dear friend, wife, brother, lover, which seemed nothing but privation, somewhat later assumes the aspect of a guide or genius; for it commonly operates revolutions in our way of life, terminates an epoch of infancy or of youth which was waiting to be closed, breaks up a wonted occupation, or a household, or a style of living, and allows the formation of new ones more friendly to the growth of character. It permits or constrains the formation of new acquaintances, and the reception of new influences that prove of the first importance to the next years; and the man or women who would have remained a sunny garden flower, with no room for its roots and too much sunshine for its head, by the falling of the walls and the neglect of the gardener, is made the banyan of the forest, yielding shade and fruits to wide neighbourhood of men.

Ambition: Sir, indeed, hast thou removed the dark scales of mine eyes, reprieving a wounded soul.
Happy am I for thee.

Compensation: My son, mercurial is she; now she is, the soul is enraptured, then is not, the soul is embittered. But her memories are immortal. When the harsh incubus of dread realities jostles thee upon Charon's ferry, the spirit, it shall snatch thee away high up an empyrean realm, To Fantasy Land, where may lie treasures of success. Memories of Love a carnation; a nostalgic carnation of immortal repose it is in the simulacrum of the slow and slumbering flow of Lethe. A wash by this hind-sight spring, shall obliterate all thy tormenting woes.

Ambition: Such words and truth, they roll now the healing waves unto mine soul.
Amid such great pain and loss,
Rolleth in now billows of peace.
What could I say? The loss has set aright my strayed foot!
Now Sir, I am come in search of that mysterious man called Other-Self.
Who is he and whither canst I seek him.

Compensation: The painful truth is, no one knows for sure who that mysterious man Other-Self is, nor his appearance nor his sojourn, except for his terrifying powers and great might.To cast but a shadow on the gamut of thy odyssey, t'will chill thy marrow; Thou hast to run the gauntlet of titans and demons, to brave those defying grimaces of RedSeas and stubborn Jericho walls; Only by his aegis canst thou venture. Lo! even this very ground thou stand'st is deadly!

Ambition: Sir, Romance Love did make known about a sleeping giant somewhere in that cave called within, not far from hither.

Compensation: No one who hath ever entered that cave ever came out alive to unravel it. And perhaps you should venture into it to see if the mysterious man sojourns within it. Now, be quick! Gird thyself! This strange ground a Caspian! Wield that silvern!

Ambition: The vexing mysterious Sir am I helpless,
Severing of its hydra head hath only
enhanced the assault.

Compensation: But haply meseems there is one who could cauterize the stumps. Wield that gold to invoke the master of escape and mysteries, Auto-Suggestion. Must I depart now. Bid thee well my son. Quick! Gird up thine loins! This is a deadly place!

The argonaut found solace, tranquil and hopes in the words of the wise old man Compensation, who then walked away into the tortuous valley.

Casting down then his silver ring, he was taken amaze by the appearance of a panoply.

Being aware of disaster's ghoulish delight in keeping his nose to the grind-stone, he armed himself without much ado and decided to escape the Garden without venturing into the cumbersome mysteries of Mr. Other-Self which he felt rather risky.

I conjectured in my dream that the insinuation of such an insidious presumptuousness was perhaps due to the sudden compensations of the panoply and the aegis of Auto-Suggestion.

With this new found confidence, he began walking along the rugged valley with the hope of finding a suitable place to invoke Auto-Suggestion by means of the golden ring.

As expected, trouble was soon knocking at his door with a grin for there was a gathering of dark clouds and buffeting of strong winds.

And lo, a titan, so petrifying to behold appears from one of the alleys! Ambition first stood stunned and then took confidence in his panoply.

The hideous monster stood before him.

Its name was Unemployment:

Unemployment: Who art thou and whither art thou bound?

Ambition: An émigré am I from the city of Penury,
An evil place, plenished exceedingly with miseries, defeats, failures,
          starvation and such privations that slay the spirit
          even to ponder,
          And I am bound for that wonder city of Prosperity,
          To liberate myself from this burden of want,
          And to swirl out Idols of woe from mine life,
          Like as once at prostituted Judah,
          Yahu My Strength, purged his southern throne of
          the brazen snake and baleful Asherah;
          Him also tapped the prosperity springs of Gihon and
          built the Siloam Tunnel,
          Tho' felleth he by the blows of paganic barbarians,
          Yet allowed not his enemies to rejoice.
          But rose again; lifted up by Yahweh,
          Whose retributive minister with vengeance,
          Jostled them on to the Babylonian snare,
          And then further racking at Khalute,
          In the hands of the mighty Elamites.

Unemployment: So! By this I now perceive that thou art a subject
          of his majestic highness,
          The almighty Lord Poverty,
          The king of the mighty city of Penury!
          You idiot! Traitor and cursed renegade!
          Durst thou escape thy royal king and land!
          Knowest thou not with just one deadly blow with
          mine ireful fist I can put an end to thine wild
          ambitious dreams!
          Hark, I am the governor of this place,
          Appointed by his eminence, Lord Poverty!

Ambition: True O Unemployment!
          Indeed was I born under his despotic dominion,
          But the inordinate laws imposed therein,
          Was such that no sapian could ever bare.

And the like of which that singing shepherd hath
said truly in the hallow'd vulgate,
Where rivers were turned into wilderness,
Watersprings to dry ground and **fruitful lands
into barrenness**.
As such after much forethought, decided I to migrate,
To a more amicable city, even the glorious city of
Prosperity;
That throbs with splendour as at the Valley of the
Maidens, in ancient land of Shiloh,
Wherein the Arcadian lasses by morn,
When Phoebus set'st out hauling along, the
Smiling-Fire-Ball, to transit the expanse,
Daily wake with singing hearts merrily from their
cozy beds at a waking snap of dawning harbingers,
And rush at once to greet fruit gardens, orchards
and Vineyards.

Unemployment: No king, I dare assert, would ev'r delight in losing
his men.
Sith thou complainest of such seamy conditions, I'll
help thee,
If only thou interposest thy vain purpose and yield
unto me.
I'll give thee housing facilities at a good, reasonable
rate at mine village called Mediocrity,
Which lieth not far from here, a haven.
And thou canst labour at mine plantation,
That is, the Hard Manual Labour Estate,
Managed by mine appointed manager, Mr. Tyranny.
If thou provest thyself worthy and loyal,
Then will he remove thy burdens and thou canst the
bare needs meet.
Hark and behold, the Issue of Adultery, saith in the
inspir'd Grecian Septuagint:
The sleep of a **labouring man** is sweet,
whether he eateth much or little bit,
But the wealth of the rich will not let him sleep in

peace or have sweet and happy dream.

Ambition: Such pelting songs they sang, such charming words
they spake unto his ears;
Whose great tremor, like an upshot of convection,
that pierceth asunder ev'n his body, soul and spirit,
That they might lull him away from his toil for honour.
But bound he himself firmly unto his objective and
spurned them all!
Hark thou Unemployment! This day, this hour, yea,
ev'n this very moment he standeth before thee!
Here I stand, an **Ulysses!**
Marvel not wherefore I speak this manner!
Venerate I pray thee, mine God-given prerogative of
option.
Obnoxious indeed are thy sordid, abhorred offers,
Unto mine inner cravings for fame, gold, recognition
and big accomplishments.
Verily could I seek refuge from thy infernal wrath at
the Hard Manual Labour Estate,
And receive the security of food, shelter and clothes
at Mediocrity.
But then meseems, there's more height to life than to be
absorbed into the maelstrom of ceaseless struggles;
To cadge for the basic necessities of life and to be
bound by the thralldom of drudgery.
For mine heart is set upon the Cornucopia, offered
so freely in the glorious city of Prosperity.
Prosperity!
How it thrilleth mine lorn heart!
Prosperity!
Like wooing arrows of a cluster of **reddish
Anemones** that slay tourists.
City of Prosperity!
'Tis a haven!
T'will be like reposing' by the sweet bank of fam'd
Jordan River, at Dagonia,
Whereat majestic **Tamarisk Trees** fan their

sheltering, rustic branches to cool a weary, thirsty soul.

Unemployment: A truism 'Tis indeed, but nev'rtheless, to conjure the complete realization of thy perception of the blind alley,

Wherein 'gainst Sagacity thou hast been led by thy whimsy, foolish ambitious dreams,

I shall herenow enlighten thy knowledge, that thou may'st make from utter perdition:

Many block-headed argonauts like thee, who hath repudiated the security of mediocrity life to venture forth in this foolish odyssey,

By reason of the alluring offers of the horn of Plenty, glory and recognition,

Did alas walk into their own obsequies;

Conducted by the Reverend Disaster and **Pastor Fates**, with none but **Mr. Death** to bemourn them.

Hark thou O argonaut,

This painful exemplary should provide food for some profound thought.

Hark, not to mention of the many whom I had personally hauled, whipped and brutally tortured and slain and chopped to pieces, amid their progress!

Thy ears must have surely seen,

And thy eyes must have surely heard,

Of gory news of countless, who were scotched and crucified upside-down, reaching their bitter haven of an ignomious bane!

Hast thou not heard, you filtered Idiot!

That durst have the effrontery to defy Lord Poverty, me and our kingdom's laws!

It strikest me now!

Thy fellow citizen, from Penury, Mr. Never-Give-Up and his poor dear family are now waiting a brutal execution the next rest,

Pending his own decision to give up his wild dreams and to settle in peace at mine village, Mediocrity,

And labour at hard Manual Labour Estate.
Wherefore, harken unto mine counsel my good friend;
The security I offer is brighter than a blind venture
and a certain death.
The true contentment I hereby offer shall suffice
thee and thy family.
So then, wilt thou not rest upon my good laurel?

Ambition: Nay titan nay!
To feed me with such Lotus,
That I might forget mine rightful cravings,
Thou shalt but flounder O Unemployment!
'Tis true, but by virtue of their failure to recognize
the great Sage of Concord,
And his eternal laws, many hath perished.
Nor did they ever endeavour to seek and to invoke
the powers of that strange, mysterious man, Mr.
Other-Self.
For depths neath me lieth a fiery burning coal;
An unquenchable burning obsession!
And a thousand water of disaster,
Canst never never douse that fire!
All thy mediocrity offers have I weighed against
desires and wants of mine heart,
But the latter did weigh sore heavily.
Wherefore have I thus persuaded myself to venture,
despite all dread dangers.

Unemployment: O stark ignorant Fool!
Art thou not read in Philosophy?

Ambition: Yea O titanic pedant, not just read, but have critically
anatomized it.
Breakforth that we may vie.

Unemployment: Hast thou not reckoned, O Fool the great words of
the anathematized lens grinder, who, spurned the
tutorial throne of Heidelberg,

That he might abide at mine village:

"After I had learned from experience that everything that repeatedly occurs in everyday life is futile and fruitless and had seen that the things of which I was afraid were neither good nor bad intrinsically but only in so far as the mind is affected by them . . . I was aware of the many advantages that come from fame and fortune and knew I would have to abstain from seeking them if I wanted seriously to pursue something new and different; and I recognized that if it should turn out that the highest happiness did reside in fame and fortune it would be bound me by. On the other hand if it did not so reside and I devoted myself to them. Then again I should fail to attain the highest happiness."

Doth not the passion for wealth, fame depict Dante's wolf! Wherefore callow the satiation of pleasure, leadeth to woe and heartbreaks rather than to the blessed life. For events, like as these harsh realities thou seest now are in accordance to fixed laws. Wherefore, despise not mine offers lest thou reapest wrath. Discover sublime root of eye-opener at mine estate and village.

Ambition: Let me refute, or rather elucidate,the tuberculosis
              Victim's conceit by the premises of Epicurus solely;

Doth not the pursuit of all pleasure fall into two categories-the natural and the unnatural, the necessary and unnecessary. Wherefore the former is sublime and honourable. For 'Tis void of selfishness, greed and every manner of perverse inclinations and evils, which flourisheth mordantly in the latter, wherefore in the pursuit of the former, surely, one can nev'r incur divine wrath.

> Thy incriminating attribution of evil to mine
> obsession for fame and fortune mocketh the very
> premise upon which Thou stand'st;
> Hark, for intrinsically according to Spinoza, my
> desir's are not evil.
> For I enjoy sublime pleasure, in the pursuit of fame

and gold,
Which is, but the alpha and omega of the blessed life.

Unemployment: Look now argonaut, perhaps according to thy
Epicurus, thy obsession is not at all evil.
But the Logos, surely condemneth thy evil pursuit,
Would'st thou defy the Holy writ!
Hark now:

'But they that will be rich fall into temptation and a snare and into many foolish and hurtful lusts, which drown men in destruction and perdition. For the obsession for prosperity is the root of all evil; which while some coveted after, they have erred from the faith, and pierced themselves thro' with many sorrows. Therefore thou argonaut, flee these things; and follow after righteousness, godliness, faith, love, patience, meekness which thou canst find at mine estate and village'.

Wherefore O argonaut, make from the road to the
city of Prosperity.
Hark, labour not to be rich!

Ambition: But thou forget'st O Unemployment,
While the Logos warneth of the abuse of Yahweh's
wealth,
It also enlightens us on its positive values.
Doth not the Logos say, that all riches and wealth
are Divine gifts;
He shall give riches, wealth and honour,
His blessing maketh rich, He shall, fill thy barns
with plenty.
He giveth power to get wealth, he desires above all
things, that we prosper,
He even challenges to open His windows and flood
us with prosperity.
Herein O titan is the positive value of the city of
Prosperity which I have set upon;
That He bids me to sow bountifully that I may

abound to every good work.

Unemployment: But a tormenting truth I have for thee;
                 The Almighty hath never chosen thee for fame and
                 fortune.
                 Is it not written; the Lord maketh poor and the Lord
                 maketh rich,
                 Two men in town, one rich, the other poor,
                 He shall not be rich.
                 Hark, all men surely are not created equal;
                 For some he hath made them wealthy Philemons,
                 While others, He hath humbled them to be Useful
                 Slaves.
                 Thou art not created for Prosperity but for Mediocrity
                 and Hard Manual Labour Estate!

Ambition: Hath not the Swan of Avon brought this truth by fat
                 Falstaff's boastful mouth,
                 That homo the word for Man!
                 Cruel distinctions amongst Homo Sapians arose from
                 that bad tree of the knowledge of good and evil.
                 I defy thee O Unemployment,
                 That there's shadow of turnings in the good Creator;
                 The portal of His infinite Heart is ever open, both to
                 a forlorn Destitute Man and a majestic patrician.

Unemployment: Ha, Ha, ha O fool!
                 Thou shalt anon see if He will come unto thy aid
                 when I barbeque thee!
                 Or if the Stars will hide indeed their fires to blind
                 the dread perils that lurk before thy road to fame
                 and gold thou off-headed Macbeth!
                 O stupid mule!
                 Reckon O reckon, thou stiff-neck rebel, the dangers
                 that await thee!

Ambition: What! Shall He not hasten when Him I call!
                 Verily verily He will! That thou wilt see!

The dangers have I reckoned,
But no fear standeth before this juggernaut of bold
Venture!
'Tis the fourth man amidst fiery trials!

Unemployment: Venture despite certain death!

Ambition: Yea O Unemployment! In this matter reckon me a
             Palamon;

'I that loveth so hote Amalthea the brighte,
That I wol dye present in hir sighte
Therefore I axe deeth and my juwyse'

I trust mine obsession and it shall attain the purpose
at all cost,
If not, my death be my repose!

Unemployment: O argonaut, vent not thy foolishness,
             By leaning upon thy heart's obsession,
             It is like that unstable Fire Ring,
             The sore heartbreaks it shall vest upon thee,
             Shall outshadow all lights of its glories.
             Reckon O argonaut, that monument of heartbreak
             and sorrow upon that deep;
             First, it did seem right for him to place trust upon
             his only issue;
             The recipient of many worthy and envied honours.
             Alas! came a victory shrouded in black sails,
             That threw the good old king into the deep,
             That till this day standeth an Aegean sea!
             Hark, the man whom thou call'st Other-Self shall
             bring about only thy destruction.
             Reckon again that gallant swain, Troilus,
             Whose god, love and consuming obsession was that
             faithless dog, capricious Criseyde;
             Who at last betrayed him.
             In perception of his follies cried he:

'And in himself he laugh at the wo
Of hem that wepten for his deth so faste;
And dampned at oure werk that foloweth so,
The blyde lust, the which that may not laste,
And sholden at oure herte on hevene be caste.

Thine blind ambitions will not last and shall betray
thee.
Accept mine offers and save thyself from all
disappointments.
Thou art a mortal callow,
Wherefore thou hear'st not the music sublime of the
concentric Heavens.
Hark unto me therefore, for speak I from the pure
realm which Troilus himself at last entered.
Trade thine ass O argonaut!

Ambition: Thy twinning meanders appeareth more beautiful
and beguiling than even the **Cani-River of Pheonica**!
Think'st thou O titan, of alluring me into thine
meandering sophism?
An imbecile fool am I not nor ever to incline unto thy
sophism!
Which by my pan, a conception of thine fiendish
instinct to debase and to ultimately destroy mine
soul at Mediocrity.
Yea, reckon Arcite after Amazon Victor severed
him from his obsession and sent him away to a
mediocrity village that highte Thebes;

'So much sorwe had never creature
That is, or shall, whyl that the world may dure.
His sleep, his mete, his drink is him biraft,
That lene he wex, and drye as is a shaft
His eyen holwe, and grisly to biholde;
His hewe falwe, and pale as asshen colde,
And solitarie he was, and ever allone,

And wailling at the night, making his mone.'
To hark unto thee O Unemployment,
'twill be to welcome the Promethean fate.
Rather than being chained to a sable life of mediocrity,
And having mine vitals torn and tormented by the grim
vultures of unfulfilled cravings,
I choose to die by the sword of disappointment,
And receive the quietus.
Tell me then O wise titan,
Would it be better to be tormented day and night by the
fiery burning fires of unrealized dreams than to face thy
threats?

Unemployment: O numskull!

        The virtue of thy senses hath lost its savor!

        Thy endings surely would harmonize with the
        saying:

'Out of the frying pan into the fire!'

        The torments and certain destruction that lay await
        thee,

        Shall make thee declare the Procrustean torture of
        being only too gracious and merciful!

        O graceless! Amid that bed when thou shalt howl for
        help,

        No god or angel would ev'r come nigh thee!

        But alas, O argonaut; 'twill be too late!

        O, foul not thy nest while Time smileth still.

Ambition: Wonder is thy words, that could even light up
        lignaloes!

        Hath the seven springs ev'r failed the Thames? Nay!

        Behold the despotic Tree that sprouted up higher
        and higher for four score and three years.

        Tho' fell he neath the dew of heavens for seven long
        years,

        Yet the Source restored him.

        Even so the Source will never, never fail nor forsake
        me!

Under the Azure Vault,
Doth not mercies of great providence bloom?
Yea! Wherefore I fear no evil!
For mine confidence reposeth upon the immutable
laws of the wise old man.

Unemployment: **Lo, the Rugged Voice** which once did herald His
purpose and great will;
In such valour and intrepid bellows vaulted he up,
As to make even the welkin tremble and ring.
Alas! what was his recompense?
Upon the dark Fortress of Machaerus did grim
Atropos sheared apart the thread!
Where was his Source then!
Harken now thou fool;
No one, not even Him, the Almighty could turn the
captivity set upon thee by the **triad Sisters**;
'Tis irrevocably fixed, thy doom!
Now! Take heed thou Sisera,
Set not the dread river Kishon in spate by thine
contumacy!
I warn thee set not!
Wilt thou not yield without further ado!

Ambition: Now, allay thy tempest Mr. Titan!
Is it not written, in the Septuagint;
Be not hasty in thy spirit to be angry: for anger rests
in the bosom of fools.
Thy astolpho-horn maketh not a taint upon mine
buckler,
For mine confidence resteth upon that mysterious
man who alone could save me from thy power,
Yea deliver me from all snares, even Fate!

Unemployment: Truth say I unto thee;
No one knoweth who the mysterious man, Other-
Self is.
Lord Poverty and I went to no end, In seeking him, by

reason of soothing our curiosity and to destroy him;
But thus far we were only confounded.
Me-seems, he may never really exist
Wherefore, dream to thy heart's bent, thou dung-head!
Thy Other-Self shall appear unto thee as like the
dead sons by Usher's Well!
Now, harken unto mine heeds;
The tempest regardeth not **a portly Argosy**
Nor a **gallant Galleon!**
Lo! The twilight is closing in fast!
And before Black Death dickers over thy soul,
Receive mine words and yield thyself unto Mediocrity
and Hard Manual Labour Estate!

Ambition: O threatful titan! Twirl not thine mustache!
Perhaps I may never him find or know,
But nevertheless have I confidence upon mine
panoply to fence myself!

Unemployment: Ha, ha, ha! Flaunt not thyself O numskull,
In the fragile and worthless panoply!
It is a mere Piccaninny's play thing!

Ambition: Tosh! Ash upon thy haughty laughter thou
contemptible titan!
Seemingly tho', yet with this fragile panoply will I
take thee by the sling and five stones!

Unemployment: Hoist not mine dander . . .

Ambition: O foppish titan! How must I effectuate thy
recognition of thine own foolishness!
Wherefore . . .

Unemployment: I warn thee fuel not the fire . . .

Ambition: Tosh! Foolish titan! Wherefore persist thou sore
frivolously in spinning the woeful yarn,

When it falls short of the hermetic seal of mine citadel!
Avaunt I warn thee!
Try not mine patience I warn thee again!

Unemployment: You bastard! Son of a lame donkey! Son of a bitch!
Most worthy to be hewn and strewn upon that
Euxine deep!
Durst thou parade arrogance before thy master!
By the time I am thro' with thee, the hermetic seal
would be found no more,
And **thou'll go crawling and kissing the dust, to Canossa!**
Take heed you rascal! Son of an ass!
Tamper not with the lid of the seething cauldron of
mine infernal wrath!

Ambition: You Gila Monster! Son of Gorgon!
Most worthy and fit to fall by Beowulf's sword!
Refine your address before I tutor thy tongue!
For I'm a knighted argonaut!
And is to be called Sir, Ambition!
Make from; I warn thee! The rumbling juggernaut of
obsession!
I hereby flout thy laws! Thee! And that fiendish beast
Poverty!

Unemployment: Roar! You blithering idiot!
Godes yrre baer!
Thou hast knocked open the Pandora's Box!
O the twisting vortex ariseth now!
Ah! Cold Boreas and cozy air!
Their tryst anon at the Gulf!

Ambition: You abominable Yahoo! (draws out his sword)
Mine indignation standeth upon zenith!
Think'st thou I fear thee! My foot!
My sword craveth for fray!
Wherefore delayst thou in taking up the gauntlet

you empty vessel!
Come out of the coop you chicken!
And face me with your trident rather than words!

Unemployment: You waspish weakling! Whoreson! Son of a dog!
Unworthy for mine feeble finger!
Durst thou challenge me! You dog!
Durst thou warn me! You loon!
I swear now by the vengeful River!
That Time shall anon wake to find thee tame!
Behold! The guardian of this valley,
Mine faithful servant, Suicide!
Shalt now try thy mettle!

Chapter 4

Sir Ambition Battles hideous Giant Suicide

With this, Unemployment bellowed out a mighty roar that resounded far and wide till the entire place tremored. Lo, out of a nether lair arises a **hideous giant called, Suicide,** whose striking horror could transfix even Hercules to a wall of fear and hopelessness!

Like a starving Harpy it now gazes ravenously upon its victim! My good Lord! This is terrible!

The hope of recovering even a tiny fragment of his bone or hair burns away in the fiery heat of the giant's grasping look, brandishing club and cyclopean strides as it made towards him. In an ominous precognition I beheld in my immortal dream of this Progress, Ambition's wraith, and I wept much for my hero;

"After venturing thus far from Penury should this be the end of the good man! O the Good Lord of heavens and earth, almighty creator of all that is good and pure, in whom there's no shadow of turnings!"

"Will not thy anointing fall upon the good man's panoply as it did in the days of yore upon that shepherd boy's sling and five stones!"

In the brink of this approaching disaster I was to gape at another astounding sight (perhaps in answer to my cries): all of a sudden, Ambition's panoply shone and radiated in iridescent glitters as if it has come to life! Then did the argonaut feel a strange wave of power surging thro' his entire body from the top of his head to the sole of his feet; the reverberation of which sparked off an inner cataclysm thus rekindling every being and cell with fiery flaming passion which truculently cried out to greet the infernal challenge.

Not being able to contain he hoisted his sword (called the sword of persistance) and erupted in a volcanic fury, screaming:

"For I am the master of my Fate and the captain of my soul!"

With this battle cry he ran forward like a charging mad bull, brandishing his passionate sword and like the explosive crashing of two irresistible rolling boulders from two high mountains they crashed against each other in such fearful impact.

Like sparing gladiators locked up in a horrible duel of death they exchanged, biffed such terrifying, deadly blows-such powerful blows that could have flatten ten sequoias or oaks with one strike!

I stood baffled in retrospect to behold the wretched man who once dandled in inferiority complex and timidity at the streets of Penury metamorphosed into a paragon of valiant gladiator; vociferously battling with such jaunty leaps and indignant groans.

Even the valley could not endure the weight of this battle; for the sore combat flaring up horrendously to its apex not only had catastrophic repercussions, whereby the place tremored, loosening, shattering the mountains, but also obliterated the raging argonaut's awareness of huge ravaging boulders that fell rumbling down the valley so precariously.

The duel battle cauterized with such shocking fury and mind staggering violence obviously would have defied even the combined efforts of hell, earth and heaven to stop them!

But even amidst the gruesome fight and in the devastating storm of his seemingly berserk wrath he remained the arbiter of his unconquerable soul and held a sense of humour.

At one stage, standing aloft a rock (which was fragmented from an unlucky gargantuan rock that received Suicide's missed aim), brandishing his bloodied sword he pounced savagely in a leonine ferocity upon the giant, thunderously yelling: "Yaarr!"

The head on crash brought about a mighty stand-still by the gluing of their assailing weapons crossed, throwing them on to their mettle as they pulled up gnashing their teeth every jot of their being and strength to depress their respective weapons against the other, sideward.

Ambition was first put in cart when Suicide by its brute strength swayed his sword down to the side blazoning the gain of an upper hand with a raucous laughter. Bereft of the hope of making a sally, Ambition being thrown on the rack earnestly persevered.

Suddenly, by a strange hoisting of that potent rod, he began countervailing the giant's might, swayed and depressed its club down the opposite side, at the same time bellowing out the victorious laughter, which made Suicide blush with shame.

Notwithstanding the humiliation Suicide counter-whelmed and bringing their crossed weapons centre between their faces they leaned forward In the static impact, scowling viciously at each other; Suicide tickled by the thought of having the game in its hand, superciliously pressed forward its grisly face, and arrogantly laughed haughtily: "Har har har!"

But Ambition in emulation inclined his resolute face even closer, retorted sardonically: "Hee, hee, hee." Bewildered and shocked, Suicide pulled its face away in disgust.

But again leaned forward, this time threateningly roared thunderously to intimidate him. But Ambition defiantly pressed his face even closer and made an insolent grimace and thumbed his nose at the giant.

This was enough; the giant exploded in rage, broke the standstill and they plunged right into seething combat.

At another time when Ambition was in cart, he retreated upwards a mountain to strategically notch up against the giant's advance, battling bloodily till they reached the summit.

Biffing with all their might, the deadly clash of their weapons brought again a crossed standstill but giving a mighty round swing, their assailing weapons slipped, flew from their hands down the mountain.

Suicide espying a nearby boulder lifted and hurled viciously at him, which Ambition shielding himself with his escutcheon (called self-confidence) fell on his back dazzled, as his shield slipped off fell down the mountain.

But at once in an antaean might the hero flung himself forth, grappling the giant with his bare hands like a bear they barbarically wrestled, tumbling down the mountain. Picking their respective weapons down the valley they went berserk and battled indefatigably with such dumbfounding violence and bristling fury!

Many atimes Suicide uprooted trees, huge boulders and even craggy rocks to missile him down. But Ambition's escutcheon proved to be a worthy bulwark.

This horrible non-stop battle lasted for six days six nights devastating almost the entire valley.

No man could imagine or apprehend its horrendous extend unless he had personally witnessed like me.

But the sombre climax smiled upon the odious giant Suicide, as the antaean argonaut yawed from mother earth, floundered, tattered and bleeding to hold back the mighty Behemoth's brutish advance.

Notwithstanding the giant's hail storm bludgeoning, Ambition's escutcheon and sword gave way and he fell dazzled and worn, unable to arise while Suicide whetted the final blow to finish off the good man.

Then did the poor hero began despairing his life.

Now, as the bellowing Suicide and **grinning Unemployment** stood before the fallen man:

Ambition: O Suicide, wherefore linger thy hand
            Upon the accursed of God!
            Let fall the club of mercy!
            Rid the gabbage of this world.
            Remove this thorn from the Almighty's heart!

As Suicide hoisted its club, a strange man interjected the fateful moment, commanding it to hold back. His name was Mr. Failure who seemed to be a close aide to the governor.

He then hinted the suggestion of serving the argonaut with ghastly examples of tortures so as to make him yield willfully.

Unemployment pleased at the proposal stripped him of his armor, bound and dragged him along while Suicide flogged him from behind.

He was hauled pass in the scourge the mysterious cave of Within, the sight of which reminded him of his beloved redeemer-the mysterious man, Mr. Other-Self who laid in a great slumber unknowing of his predicament.

But shrilling thoughts of the confused mysteries enshrouding him turned it to a forlorn hope.

He was taken into the garden's castle called Despond and imprisoned. He was also led into the castle's torture chamber, to meet his former friend and neighbour

Mr. Never-Give-Up who was then undergoing a gruesome torture by being bound to two wooden pillars and flogged by the castle's guards.

The iron-willed man smilingly told him that rather than relinquishing his aspirations to drink of the fountain of knowledge and settle in the village called Higher Education in the city of Prosperity, he delights in the mutilated body of his and in the whippings.

The fateful day for Mr. Never-Give-Up and his family came the following week when he had to appear before Unemployment's throne to voice his decision as to whether he wanted to accede to Lord Poverty's terms in renouncing his aspirations, to settle at Mediocrity and labour at Hard Manual Estate or to face a brutal death.

Being inured to the torture by virtue of his iron will, he walked boldly into the trial hall in an aura of perseverance, took a defiant stance before the Governor, the Garden's chief officials and dignitaries from Penury.

Then, in fiery gestures, the hardy Mr. Never-Give-Up let loosed a stream of nerve shattering invectives, inveighing in a stentorian tone against Lord Poverty and his laws.

Notwith-standing the renting philippic the officials and dignitaries tore their garments in rage, crying out for his immediate death.

Unemployment sentencing the enraged man, his wife, teenage daughter and the little kid to death ordered them to be hauled to the execution hill called Imbroglio Highlands.

Amid the frantic pleas for mercy and help the brutal guards jostled them. Ambition was also present at the Highlands.

Such was the horror of the brutal, torture-murder that I had to close my eyes in the dream.

Nevertheless I shall describe briefly. But even now as I write, I am petrified, for the lurid orgy of the carnage haunts me like Medusa's evil gaze.

The poor man and his wife were tied to a stake while one of the guards held the boy.

Unemployment summoned **the giant Suicide**, who came, picked up the screaming girl by her feet and in a mighty swing dashed her against a nearby rock;

as her head shattered into bloody pieces, spattering the place with blood no tongue could describe the shrieking screams of the parents and the kid who went berserk with convulsive shock.

The giant then renting her apart, devoured ravenously. Ambition could only struggle in vain with the guards to save the girl.

Following this as Unemployment caught hold of the terrified boy and began severing his arms and legs, the fathomless heaven could not contain nor could the deepest ocean drown the frantic screams of the parents.

What a heartless, heinous effrontery it was when the castle's guards and officials burst into a delirious clamour when the freakish body of the armless and legless boy tumbled about the pool of blood in convulsion.

Grapping a spear, the brutal monster, impaled the boy by the neck.

Oh, the eye blinding horror followed next! His wife was gang raped!

Ambition at this stage fell prone burying his face on to the ground crying feverishly while the husband went berserk, screaming and bellowing over his might, frothed vomiting greenish froths.

Taking hold of her mutilated, dying body the monster plunged its bloody dagger into her belly tearing it open, hooking out the bowels which gushed out onto the ground.

And the poor husband concussed violently till blood gushed out of his nose and mouth!

The saga of Mr. Never-Give-Up's torture began next. The guards first thrashed him up, gouged out his eyes and sliced off his tongue.

Skinning him next, they poured brine and whipped. In the brutal bedlam the poor man wriggled, tumbling about venting such piercing screams.

When Unemployment impaled by the neck, he violently gasped.

And thus the brave Mr. Never-Give-Up, finally gave up his ghost and dies the most cruel and horrible death one could ever imagine.

Ambition being petrified by the brutality succumbed and fell prostrate before Unemployment's feet pleading for mercy:

Ambition: I implore thee o mighty governor!
              Abate thy wrath, for I hereon renounce mine will and bury all mine obsessions!
              O mine follies,
              I repent bitterly in ash and sackcloth!
              A blind fool am I;
              Like a presumptuous Poetaster who flaunts before the lettered Virtuoso,
              So have I arrayed such words I knew not against thee!
              O I beseech thee lord!
              Will not mercy canopy this weeping, penitent heart that importunes the master's feet?
              Prithee!
              Spurn me not, I beg, plead and implore thee,

With a pardon denied precipitate,
That brought headlong the **third rebellious hosts.**

Unemployment: Arise thou, O crestfallen paupernaut!
Take heart I say, all is well.
Now, make haste,
Flee unto Hard Manual Labour Estate!
By thy faithful compliance therein wilt thou live with impunity.
Hence, canst thou remove all thy burdens of want.

Ambition: My merciful master!
How mine heart leaps,
To come without this clay-trunk to thank thee!
Rest assured my master, mine faithfulness shall set thine pass-over.

And I awoke from my sleep. What a horrifying nightmare it was!

The torture, the killing and the brutality were all so vivid!

Soon I felt drowsy; slept, and drifted back to my immortal dream.

Chapter 5

Sir Ambition Imprisoned In Hard-Manual—Labour-Estate

ehold, at Hard Manual Labour Estate he meets the manager, Mr. Tyranny:

Tyranny: Thy yarn doth arouse mine pity for thee.
                    Thou need'st not strife nor labour that far,
                    Which by mine conceit, utter foolishness;
                    For it doth expose thee to much perils,
                    Here, if thou wert to humbly submit,
                    Then wilt thou the good harvest see and reap.

Ambition: Good master, the yoke will I gladly bear.
                    I shall flog this oxen to its mettle,
                    This be thou assured, until it merits thy entire confidence and thy honour.
                    Master, once had I lofty vanity,
                    But now is no more;
                    To please and esteem thee and the great governor of Sorrow alone,
                    Shall be mine obsession hence forth;
                    I shall nev'r betray the good security,
                    Thou hast bestowed upon this poor cipher.
                    Now Sir, I cannot tarry to serve thee,
                    Quickly bid thy servitor and vassal.

Tyranny: Such submissive proclivity thou display'st,
                    Is indeed a commendable virtue.
           Some worthy instructions must thou receive;
           Now incline to the letters;
           In no wise should'st thou despise or spurn the chastisement of thy superiors,
           For they are to whet thy character of such mould as to gloze thee.
           Thou should'st always be happy with the lot vested upon thee by the Almighty,
           Including the most dirtiest, abhorred jobs;
           Thy sojourn hither is in harmony with that blesseth plan and all-wise purpose,
           Hark, t'was never, not 'Tis now nor ever will be Divinity's pleasure to drench thee in excess with abundance or wealth,
           That will only make thee arrogant, proud,
           And lead thee into diverse perversions.
           His will is for thy basic wants be met.

Ambition: Yea Sir, I've giv'n ear unto thy counsels,
           Be assured Sir, even the harshest behests,
           Shall never disaffect this servitor.
           Now Sir, what be mine work?

Tyranny: Hark, we grow trees hither called, Quietism;
           The fruit it yields is Mental-Atrophy.
           Thy quotidian duty is to harvest these valuable fruits and meet our quotas,
           As thy pay is dependent upon this.
           Unto thy senior bailiff, Mr. Flay, art thou required to report and submit.
           He, Mr Flay shall guide and instruct thee,
           In the work thou hast to perform daily.
           Now, an important heed thou hast to note;
           In work matters, I rule with iron rod,
           Wherefore in nowise incur mine anger by any unworthy, poor performance.

	All to be done effectively and fast.

All to be done effectively and fast.
Art thou clear?

Ambition: Yea Sir! Right to the needle's eye, I'm clear!
Sir! From the lighting of the World-Candle,
To melting of it, will I flog myself to serve thee,
To plough thy fields and to fly thy errands.
Nor will the ev'r watchful glass slumber amid its delighted duty,
While perpetual incense shall ever fog and cloud the affected tabernacle.
Sir! Let this body be hammered, pounded and thrown upon as a rosy carpet for thy venerable feet to tread upon!

Tyranny: Now, hasten to make good thy confession!

I beheld him in my dream labouring at that abhorred plantation the Hard Manual Labour Estate.

How he laboured to the consuming heat of his might.

Sweating himself out in the blazoning sun, harvesting and shouldering huge bunches of fruits upon his bare back.

Well, nothing but the crooked obsession to prove himself worthy to his evil masters, to rid of his burden of want and to gain recognition could have stretched him to the near snapping point of his body, soul and spirit.

In consternation wondered I, against his better judgment shrouded by illusive and diabolical indoctrination wrought about by the villains, what intrinsic factor blinded him into such foolish acquiescent; I dare assert, it was that crushed ego within him which was the consequent of his confrontation with the formidable Governor of Sorrow, Unemployment.

Yes, though he now lives and labours yet he is stark dead! His inner man or spirit has been crushed to a cruel death. He laboured and endured the gruesome burden of Hard Manual Labour Estate as an insane man one who is oblivious to his true dignified heritage, and self-esteem.

Yet fell he short of their expectation and favour; for he was berated by his superiors over trivialities. Such grilling worthy of animals or rather inanimate stones he had to now stoically endure. Nor were his colleagues any greener. In my dream it seemed as though he persevered under this antagonistic ambience day after day, week after week, month after month till he grew weaker and weaker.

Despite such simmering conditions he slacked not a scintilla in his unabated endeavour to prove himself worthy, for he was convinced that the all wise plan and purpose was chaperoning his course. In short, the word, hope beyond the plantation did not exist nor will it ever for him.

Mr. Tyranny angered by Ambition's poor performance, ordered him to be closely scrutinized by two foreman, Mr. Reproach and Mr. Condemnation who then kept his nose to grind stone and even made him haul and bear huge stones for road construction work.

One night at his lodge in Mediocrity, he began discussing his predicament with his senior work mates, Mr. Hard-Work. Mr. Fatalist and Mr. Start-Bottom:

Ambition: My good friends, I know not what I can do to make mine ends meet or to gain recognition.
And now, I've incurred our Reeve's displeasure.

Hard-Work: Take mine advice friend, that thou mayest rid thy burdens, frustrations and troubles.
The way thou could'st please our good manager,
Is to show, enhance thy productivity.
There lieth a mount at our plantation, called, Mount Overtime,

Wherein prized trees grow known as Drudgery,
yielding fruits called Chagrin;
These fruits fetch a high wage, and hence thy wage
and productivity shall surely increase.

Ambition: Behold my good friend! With mine ebbing strength
how am I to labour there!

Fatalist: Don't be a fool! When lady luck spurned us amidst
a life's wreck;
In that fuming brine, a stoical plank is our only
hope.
Wherefore despise not the hardships my friend,
'Tis our only haven of survival.

S. Bottom: In these gloomy days one has to begin at the bottom
and work his way up.

And thus inclining to the pessimistic words of the dullards he
headed straight into that ravine of utter dismay. Labouring at Mt.
Overtime he at last realized the Sisyphean task he had embarked
upon; for no sooner he had harvested the fruits and brought it
down the mountain than it rotted away.

Towards the evening, seeing a wasted mess and an unmet quota,
Mr. Reproach and Mr. Condemnation brutally whipped and kicked
the frail man till he collapsed in a pool of blood.

Day after day thereafter he was caviled, slapped and whipped till
he withered away to just skin and bones.

One day the foreman after beating him up as usual, hauled him to
the manager's office and on their way:

Ambition: O ye merciless brutes! Cruel ruffians!
Doth mine torments fan your ghoulish instincts!
Wherefore maul ye a poor dying cipher!
Whose lorn transit is but as a flower, that blooms in

the morn and withers away by even.

Reproach: Durst thou speak! You idiotic fool! Numskull!
Bottle-sucking piccanining! Slothful bloke!
Dung-headed! Shoddy dumb-bell! One more word,
from thy most detested, stuttering mouth,
I'll daub thy gorge raising visage with dung!
Plough up thy condemned trunk and dislocate
everyone of thy abhorred joints for dogs!

Ambition: Call'st thou me, this knighted argonaut,
With names that would make even beasts decry!
O the twinge of it killeth me! Alas!
Wherefore didst Thou enfeeble me so soon amid that
battle!
Else would I have slain both the titans!
O that mine mighty strength hath remained,
I would have graphed these weaklings and hurled
with such might that ye would have gone crashing
thro' Pluto's throne!
Alas! Alas!
Answer me! Speak! Wherefore gavest Thou me,
The Garment of Nissus—that razed mine life!
Even so now, wherefore baulk'st Thou still in helping
me, to turn mine captivity!
O, will not the severed mane grow?
Where be mine lost powers?
Where be mine lost might?
Where be mine lost honour?
Oh! Where be mine lost life!

Condemnation: You lame brained bawdy ass! Forked tongue viper!
Ingrateful dog! Son of a skunk! Toad! Pig!
Insolent Baboon! Dirty Philistine!
Mongolian! Goat! Son of a withered whore!
Saturn whipped, cursed barbaric bloke! Idiot!
Filtered idiotic numskull! Wastrel! Bastard!
Animal-Sapian freakish son! Stupid mule!

Unworthy ev'n for tartarus! Whose corpse,
Abhorred ev'n by earth!
Whose distorted mien,more uglier than even that
dread mother and son the ArchFiend confronted in
Hell!
One more time thou dar'st exchange with words
thou diest for it!

Ambition: O the ugliest tongue, the darkest tongue,
Met by the petrified eyes of mine ear!
May fire and brimstone be teemed upon it!
May the one-eyed smiths of bellowing shafts,
Speed up their production, all to be shot and arrowed
upon thy crude, vicious sword!
May all the fieriest Locus of this orb,
Come riding by the chariot of Eurus,
To prey upon thy unruly member!
May all the plagues of the curse of the law,
Be multiplied a hundred megatime,
And be hailed upon thy dirty bad tongue!
O the wickedness of it transcendeth the abominable,
cursed, evil mysteries of the baleful witch goddess,
Hecate!
O the brutality of it outshadows even murderous
Medea and Brutus!
Alas! **Alas! He hath permitted me to be gored
fatally** by such ugliest the most wicked and the
most brutal sword of all ages; The thrust of which
even, Immortals could not endure!

Condemnation: Thou Echo possessed rotten old yarn spinner!
Hear this thou breached pot!
Perhaps the immortals may not endure this, but
thou certainly have to! (They thrash him up)

At Tyranny's office:

Tyranny: Lo! the dossier presenteth unto me by thy lords,
              Can make even stocks and stones vent its spleen
              and 'rouse the devil within!
              Look! Three fold charges are brought against thee!
              Firstly, thy work here a provoking snail!
              Speak now! Wherefore the slowness!

Ambition: Most venerable master, and my good Lord,
              The mystery, (even the thought troubleth me) of mine
              ebbing thews and sinews of late doth not unfold.
              Alas my good master, mine physical strength, mine
              only trusteth crutch, turneth a Judas!
              Master . . .

Tyranny: Durst thou speak in sweet icy metaphors,
              Sweeter than even quenching Marsala, to ravish
              mine heart! You indolent dolt!
              Further more, it was also brought to light,
              By our good Argus-eyes which we hath placed
              bountifully in our estate and lodge,
              That thou didst seek to turn thy fellowmates against
              us!
              Dost thou need mine sympathy!
              Here! Take this! (slaps him.)

              Ambition falling down, cries out:

Ambition: 'Breakforth thy virtues! O mighty Atlas!
              That I may bear this horrendous burden,
              Of grinding Hard Manual Labour Estate!'
              Master! Spared I not an unblemished lamb of loyalty
              upon mine poor alter.
              Behold, mine sacrifice in Abel's rite doth defy thy
              scourging incriminations.
              Mine faithfulness, 'twas greater than even hymenal
              bonds!

Tyranny:	You shoddy fool!
	Have thou the effrontery to vent thy justifications by evoking the esteemed titan's name, thou numskull loon!
	Hath he heard thy provoking soliloquy,
	He would have given thee a hard tight kick on thy back and then hanged thee aloft his celestial burden!
	You idiot! (kicks him)
	Mean'st thou the Clytemuestran faithfulness!
	Furthermore seeking among thy workmates,
	The faithful Aegisthusians! Durst thou talk!
	Also 'twas said; thou didst steal our prized fruits!
	Durst thou make a mockery of our kindness!
	I abjure thee now by Queen Astralea to confess thy guilt!
Ambition:	False! Most false!
Tyranny:	The most defiant perjure mine gentle ears hath ever heard!
	Swear now by Astralea and confess! I warn you!
Ambition:	Prithee Mister Reeve, know mine Tabernacle;
	Its portal open'st not, nor will ever
	Unto the gods of fabled Olympus,
	Save unto Him, even the Changeless One
	Who hath sore cruelly delivered me up into thy hands.
	Wherefore, swear I by Him;
	For the burning rod placed upon mine tongue did bring forth a fount of moisture!
	Mr. Tyranny then, renting apart his garment screams in fury:
Tyranny:	Aaar! What a horrendous perjure! Treason!
	It destroyeth mine ears! Boileth mine blood!

Liar! Wicket liar! Avaunt! Avaunt!
Thy defiant chant breaketh the gates of Hades!
You Bochica! Wherefore ease thy burden!
The earth parts! Swallowing mine gentle virtues!
Dread Medusa's blood is splashed upon me!
O the horrible Grendel is now bursting thro'
Hrothgar's hall and right into mine blood!
Fiery molten rocks are now gushing out in hideous
gusts! I'm now wax a demon!
Guards! Vanish him quick!
Before the lion rents apart its cage!

Mr. Tyranny reported this matter to the governor, who then by
way of punishment had his right eye gouged, left hand severed,
brutally whipped and mauled.
One gloomy night amidst thunder and lightning as it was about
pour he took a walk down a lonely lane nearby his lodge.

Suddenly he broke down and wept in convulsive sops.

As he wept, that strange man Mr. Think Rich came walking towards
him:

Think Rich: Bon Soir, Sir Ambition! What cheer! Alas!
              Now, what became of thee! Thy eye and arm!
              Wherefore feed'st thou upon thine vomit O mighty
              argonaut!

Ambition: Nay Sir! Call me not ev'r Sir Ambition, but Mara,
              For He hath embittered me and nipped me sore
              brutally in the bud!
              To bespeak mine sorrows, yea mine sad fate;
              Let me be cast upon Corinth's lorn shore,
              To behold in forlorn those rippling waves,
              And then cry out:
              'O, let not nor ever, that nostalgic flagrance emitting
              from thy crestful flowers pave their rueful path to

the poor hearts of these untoward souls,
Nor devour ye our disembarked Argo buried fatefully
in thine briny grave,
Remind us not of that fiendish rider of dragonish
chariot,
Who by her art, laid us to a desolate retirement'.
O Sir, Destiny hath not bidden me a bon voyage nor
the triad vixens grace.
Now Sir, behold this whilom argonaut,
Who's now a Niobe, sitting upon ash,
Wailing in utter despond and cowering,
In this dank Hard Manual Labour Estate.
Alas, I've fallen, nev'r again to arise.

Think Rich: Hark Sir Ambition, thou gallant argonaut;
Thou hast perjured before thine conscience.

Ambition: Nay Sir, thou hast yet to behold the powers and
might of that dread governor.
Behold, the manacle he has set upon me;
No power in heav'n nor on earth could break.
For mine horrid tryst with Unemployment,
'twas like a delorus stroke I received;
For it brought to a diametric shambles,
Beyond the descry of hope or redeem,
The total man of this clay-built Life-House;
The physical Kingdom, the material,
And above all mine empyreal kingdom.
Suffered mine dignity, amour proper,
A cruel death in the infernal abode,
Of Hard Manual Labour Estate,
which burns with hellish torments, fears, woes, and
sorrows.
But, was I not once a pious recluse,
Pitched within Thy holy tabernacle;
Mine eye to shun evil, and Thine favour alone to
behold,
And Thine wonder Voice, me to always cherish:

Thou mine tower, and star from mine childhood,
Yet, wherefore then Thine infinite mercy stood
strangely still,
When I did touch that fatal stormy box,
Alas, unleashing torrents of mayhem, upon mine life,
That shook me as like once;
The tempest that quaked the shores of Ithaca,
When by the folly of curiosity,
The sea-faring warriors of Odysseus,
Opened the guiding parcel of Aeolus.
Nor could I find a drowsy nepenthe,
To drown mine sorrows by which once;
The son of the crafty one did,
when given to drink by the beautiest women with a
black heart;
Wherein sprang forth evil lustful demons,
Biding her to cuckold her good husband,
To elope with old Priam's Stormy Petrel,
Him, by tampering with the angels of light,
Brought utter ruin unto the land of Troy.

Think Rich: O mighty argonaut, lift up thine eye unto the high
heavens in lieu, and lo,
Canst thou behold wonders high up there,
Which transcendeth the Terpsichorean art?

Ambition: Nay Sir, 'Tis so cloudy

Think Rich: Even so, wilt thou dispute the existence of those
wonders?

Ambition: How could'st I deny Sir!
Tho' gloomy clouds have hid mine lorn eye from the
starry lights,
Yet their existence is sure, as sure as the immutable
Law of Seedtime.

Think Rich: Harken, even so the despondent scales of thine eyes

hath now hidden the yond light,
The shining light of glorious hope,
Whose beams outshineth the morning star!
Behold now, far far off that glittering cosmic land,
the metaphysical rays shineth,
From whence thy great redeemer, the mysterious
man, the invincible Mr. Other-Self lieth in a great
mysterious slumber;
Yea he lieth thither with strange powers sans bound,
and wisdom shaming Solomon,
Wherefore thy brutal manacle shall snap like a
feeble thread before his presence.
Hark thou O Ambition, hast thou landed upon the
tormenting Isle of Aeaea,
And had thine tryst with the Enchantress,
Whereupon thou crawl'st grovelling in shame!
Behold! there'll arise one, with a molly,
Yea, to reduce to utter impotence, the potent wand
and revive thy dignity.
Project thy vision, O mighty argonaut,
Pass the gloomy, sad clouds of despondence,
Like **Esdras**, who by his vision of faith
Projected beyond his bondage and woes,
To behold and hear ecstatical songs,
Sung unto their Great Living King by them who
stripped off their mortality to don immortality!

Ambition: Embramble me not with that thorny name!
Venting of his name seteth me aflame!
What is he? Whither is he? These questions,
Nay, double edges sword slayeth me apart.
How am I to seek this invincible man?
For mine ardent pursuit being more fervent,
Than the amorous pursuit of the Sun of fleeing Daphne,
The misty daughter of Peneus.
Yea mine earnest beckoning much more ardent than
all his entreaties,
And could, but embrace her vapourized form;

Alas I now to sooth these piercing pains
With the tantalizing laurel.
But hope! Nay Sir, 'Tis pass hope for me;
For five times two score and four hours witnessed
by the Sun and the Moon while doing their celestial
chores,
Tarried I in earnest for His mercy;
As like once gallant Ozias, who withstood to endure
the same,
Till at the momentus hour, intervened the Great
Patrician of Host,
The Everlasting Hero of all Ages,
To reward his tormenting enemies,
With such shattering comeuppance.
Alas for me, 'Tis pass five waiting days and yet see
I no light.

Think Rich: O bold Ambition, hast thou fallen foul,
To the hideous Chimaeras of fear! Hark,
Doth its snorting fume of terror shrill thee!
Arise I say! Arise in the puissance of the Son of
Glaucus! Arise I say!
To mount upon the Pegasus of Faith!
For when astride this formidable winged steed,
Canst thou battle, swoop low to extort life from its
horrid form.
Arise argonaut,
Arise to seek that wonder man!

Ambition: But how Sir how! How am I to seek him!
Meseems Sir, his metaphysical mysteries are but
liken unto the Lunar Queen,
To arouse me and then to bid me make a vain
progress to the depths of lorn deep;
Alas, to roll me into the cavern of cold mount Latmus
to enwrap mine soul in chimerical fancies like that
shepherd of old, Endymion.

Think Rich: Verily verily I avouch, plight mine troth,
If thou seek'st him truly earnestly,
He'll be found of thee and thou shalt know him, even
as he really is.
Even so,
Mingle persistence with faith and obsession,
Whereof such strange wonders thou shalt behold,
Such charms, out charming the enchanting lute of
the offspring of the Sun and Calliope;
To behold as Vanquished heavens,
Throw wide her relented portals,
And Hell fling wide her consented gates,
Which did denude the terrors of the triad headed
Cani,
Humbling the Hell-Guard to a harmless fawn,
As thou goest in thy mysterious search,
Of that mysterious man, Other-Self,
In the mysterious shades.

Ambition: But now, how could'st this chap fallen argonaut lick
his fatal lesion?
Or refurbish his rankled soul, or escape this Estate?

Think Rich: Sir Ambition, thou argonaut!
You indeed started well.
But wherefore waxed thou sore foolish?
Esau's blunder hast thou made. Fie on you!
Thine birthright of that delightful city,
Hast thou exchanged for a tormenting life!
Surely the good Creator did not made thee for Hard
Manual Labour Estate!
Hast thou forgotten that golden ring I gave thee!
Invoke I say, the master of escape!
Make haste! I must leave thee. May Pollyanna's
unblemished sunshine, smile upon thee always.

Chapter 6

Sir Ambition's Escape and Discovery of the Kingdom of Within

Mr.Think Rich's words whose effect like that of the archangel's trumpet roar in the rapturous last resurrection, piercing through the squalid benighted tombstone of his soul, raised anew an argonaut out of a ciper.

Resolving to sever the Gordian knot, an escapade that would seal his death should he fail to seek and awaken that mysterious man, Mr. Other-Self. Scintillating in the gaiety of the year of Jublilee, he immediately took out the golden ring and in prudence threw it down. The stone began emitting greenish fumes and suddenly a handsome gladiator appeared, called Auto-Suggestion:

Auto-Suggestion: Good even my liege. Bid me even now;
                     Be it to scale the mountain of mystery,
                     Or break fetters of tormenting bondage,
                     Or to unlock prison gates or to head!
                     Thus mine irrevocable pledge unto thee—to be always
                     correspondent.

Ambition: Thou strange servitor, tell me if thou canst;
              Could'st thou deliver me from this sorrow,
              This bond of Hard Manual Labour Estate,
              And seek out mine lost panoply?

Auto-Suggestion: Before the wink of thine eye thou wilt exchange these sack garment for thine panoply!

Ambition: Another lacerating mystery troubleth me.

Auto-Suggestion: Make known my master.

Ambition: Know'st thou who that strange mysterious man,
               The invincible Mr. Other-Self is,
               And whither could we seek him?
               Now harken;
               By the laws that govern the four seasons,
               The tide of the deep and the firmaments,
               Of this can we be sure, that the governor of sorrow,
               that dreaded hunter, Nimrod,
               Shall relentlessly pursue his ram.
               Wherefore, should we seek out him, the mysterious
               man, Other-Self, lest we perish!

Auto-Suggestion: My good master, pardon I do beg thee,
               The truth which pains me greatly to utter
               Is that, no one knoweth who that man is,
               But nevertheless let us venture yond,
               Haply we may unravel the puzzle.

Ambition: Make haste then, let's depart in the dumbness of
               the dark.

   Enlightened and revived, his premises were now clear, though fearfully mutilated, void of a hand and an eye.

The cloudy prevision of the mystical land beyond Within could not deter him from recoursing to the sacrosanct commitment to the burning obsession of his heart which militated against the fear of jeopardizing his very life.

   Auto-Suggestion producing a white cloak hovered over and they became invisible and escaped the Estate. By way of the valley of

Broken-Heartedness, Ambition picked up his panoply and armed himself.

In fear and awe they stood on tenterhooks before the mystical cave of Within and described its cosmic interior. Jostled by hope's only gleams they then walked into its misty darkness with aplomb.

Devoid of all physical visibility except for Auto who by his intuition sturdily led the staggering argonaut by the hand till they came to a strange lake.

The name of which was called, Besetting Weakness; where patches of whirlpools were scattered and footstones ran precariously through it. In the gloomy glow of flambeaus which hung by the cave walls they ventured forth the stygian lake footstones in vigilance lest they might stumble upon some diabolical snare.

And sure enough, before they could even reach the middle, by some grievous frown of misfortune they stumbled upon a Pandora's box, knocking off its lid, unlocking the gates of Hell!

Suddenly there arose from the waters a half-man half crocodile creature (man's head, bear's hands and a crocodile's body) called Perversion which attacked and swept Ambition off his feet into the waters.

While the shock ridden man grappled desperately with the fiendish being, another grisly creature emerged, a half-man half-snake being, called Inertia, which also attacked and swirled around him.

His master's plight sparking off an inner clarion alarm to bestir himself for the momentus hour, the enraged Auto, drawing out his deadly dagger pounced barbarically upon the creatures and after a violent and petrifying fight, he smote them and rescued his master.

Upon crossing lake Besetting Weakness they came to a dead end and the discerning Auto striking the ground with his sword fell back, for there was a slight tremor. And behold the ground opened-a deep precipitous stair ran below the interior precinct. After a long tortuous descend their feet finally rested upon a plain ground much to their relief as gleams of yellowish-gold light coming from a tunnel drew their attention.

In that dusky wilderness of darkness the oasis of the afar off gleams emitting scent of hope soared up their expectancy, and they entered the tunnel.

Upon reaching the terminal they clambered out, and behold-their wonder smitten eyes see a splendour that far, far transcended the dimensions of their wildest dreams!

For before their electrified eyes was a shining kingdom of pure gold, the buildings the gates and just about everything within the sight of their roving eyes were of pure gold.

A golden shinning plate aloft the entrance gate read-kingdom of Within, guarded by a fabulous knight, who was clenching a gargantuan, beaming golden sword called Reason. His name was Sir Conscious.

Also, not far from the kingdom stood a strange mountain called Mt. Fasting amidst a wilderness known as Desperation.

In fear and trembling they then approached him:

Conscious: Who are ye?

Ambition: Hail to you dear Sir!
              Thine majestic mien, a cynosure, that humbles me
              even now for a prostrate adoration.
              I do beg, a thousand pardons for interjecting thy royal
              duty,
              For mine plight is in want of grace.

Ambition, am by name, an argonaut from the city of
Penury bound for the good city Of Prosperity.
And this, my Friday and my double-harness, Mr.
Auto,
Came we in search of that mysterious man,
The invincible Mr. Other-Self.
For learnt we by winds that he sojourneth
somewhere here. Tell us, whither might he be that
he may be found of us?

Conscious: In truth, no one wot who that man is or whither he
is.
Wherefore seek'st thou him?

Ambition: Sir, behold this maimed and wrecked house of
mine;
Abandoned by an eye and a left hand!
Should I return to the Garden alone,
That Bey of Sorrow would surely kill me.
His satanic nature and brutal deeds
Are yond comprehension, just horrendous.
Wherefore must I needs to invoke the pow'rs
Of that mysterious man, Other-Self.

Conscious: Now hearken! A callow weakling like thee,
Can win not Hope's plaudits nor be a protégé of
Fortune.
Now, return from whence ye came!
Begone! Lest I slay ye both with reason.

They left in utter disgust and though thrown in a swivel by the
guard's brusque reply Ambition was only more determined than
ever.
Auto hovered his cloak, the two then becoming invisible sneaked
pass the guard and entered, positing the hope of an aid and eying
the kingdom with a prehensile expectancy.

Auto led him through the mazes to the royal palace. Here the guards
were amiable and they were ushered in to meet the king, his royal

Highness, Lord Will-Power;

Will-Power: Welcome O argonaut! What a honour to have thee and thy companion.

Ambition: Your highness, by what virtue or reason hast thou counted it worthy to host us?
Meseems, queer is thy genial reception bestowing upon me, an unworthy man,
For even awhile ago, thy fabulous knight belittled and whipped us out.

Will-Power: What! Hath not this wonder truth dawn on thee,
That our shining kingdom is a haven and a reprieve for argonauts like thee, and to all enemies of Lord Poverty!
For this reason hath this arch adversary sent its agents to penetrate our land.
Thus far hath Sir Conscious halted them short.

Ambition: I've grasped! By reason of his suspicions hath he spurned us.

Will-Power: Yea. But how braved ye pass my guard?

Ambition: 'Tis by setting aflame the hind bridges resolved we thus.
This servitor of mine Is so amazing—he is the master of escape, and also of mysteries.
Under his cloak of invisibility we sneaked pass.

Will-Power: Good! How fared ye thro' that turbulent lake, Besetting Weakness?

Ambition: My Lord, hath it not been for mine Auto,
I would have surely boarded Charon's barge!
What a fight we hath against those monstrous beings, Perversion and Inertia!

Will-Power: T'was by thine folly!
                    Wherefore did ye cross by the footstones, rather than by taking that higher pathway by its side?

Ambition: We wist not, for it was dark,
                    Moreover, I have now but one eye to guide.

Will-Power: Those two dread creatures whom ye encountered, by day are charming damsels,
                    But by night becometh fiends which ye yourselves hath seen.
                    Hath ye but ventured by day, those beauties would have wooed ye.
                    Wherefore, many Argonauts hath miserably perished!

Like as once;
In streamy tongue and full-mooned eyes he gazed,
Not knowing of the curse he was to taste,
Tho' alarmed a voice against the temptation
Yet inclined he to steamy perversion,
Deaf ear to "Antaeon avoid lustful danger,
Avoid Selene, the queen of hunting chamber."
Alas, succumbed he to sin's horrid fetters,
Pursued by servitor hounds turned masters,
Alas, tasted that hart, that fled so sad,
By a river's edge a cruel grim death.

Beware O argonaut, of besetting lusts,
That canst stray thine objective and lead thee
into destructions.
Likewise Inertia, A deadly serpent,
Whose dread swirl could choke the very life out of thee.
And nothing but ambitious-enthusiasm alone could
drive these fiends away.

As like once by the first matrimonial night,
Of Tobias and his wedded victim racked by plight,
The sottish Asmodeus after a night's booze-up,

At Hell's bar and party wild, titillated by tough
Rutting thoughts, broke into the honeymoon room,
For his wonted impious affair-so dread and gloom.
Shocked to behold his fair slave's perfidious union,
The grim cuckold began roaring like a lion;
In combustion of spleen and contorted visage,
He rushed sabre rattling towards the groom in rage,
Unknowing of deliverance's impending sweep.
Him, the son of Tobit scotched with a fishy whip,
Brutally scourging him up before driving out;
Who notwithstanding the throes fled crashing aloud
Thro' the window, landing upon his black stallion-
Blasting off to Egypt. From a yond pavilion,
Good Raphael espying the fleeing villian, pursued
Behind, speeding upon his white horse in heroic mood.
And they raced and they raced and raced and raced:
From starry night to marmoreal mid-night;
Thro' matutinal gates, greeting Daphne
And Aurora, to smiling dawn, then
To retiring even, the pursue travailed-
Inflamed by Heaven's sore resolute will,
To wipe a forlorn soul's desperate tears.
Even elements quivered fearfully, as
The swift chase, horrid gallops, thundering hoofs,
Whirling upheavals, enraged unabated;
Thro' verdure clad dells and baren bald dales,
Skipping ov'r purling streams and deep ravines,
Beating thro' bogs, sloughs, rocks, marl and moor-land,
Pass hills, knolls, caves, plains, fells, and cataracts,
Abreast blustering storms and assailing heat,
With the swift fleeting hour then shortening
The pursuing angel's distance closer
With the fleeing fiend. When nigh Egypt's bourn,
Raphael lassoed Asmodeus, hitching down
The tormentor, who tumbled down bruising,
Whilst the holy crime-buster pounced forthwith
Upon the entrapped, impious out-law;
Grappling each other went rolling a distant.

Assayed blatantly the hell's fugitive
With his unskilled hands and legs to thwart
His capture-defending so desperately.
But let loosed the hero with artful spars,
A dread hail of deadly Kung Fu swinges-
With each blow sparking off a 'dish-dish' sound,
As the black-a-moor villain fell back wincing,
Venting in agony his 'ouch-ouch' cries.
But I tell you, not once but several times,
Did that heav'nly champion graphed the opponent,
By the scruff of his dirty rotten neck,
Dashing the hated head against a big rock.
Hark, nor didst that exciting racking end here,
But driving the vigourless foe yon stream,
Which ran thick with black slime and dung, once more,
Ducked the most detested face down and out
The muddy putrid waters, sore stenching;
With each short lived intermittent reprieve,
The villian squalling out "Yelp! Have mercy!"
Whereupon binding up, victorious Raphael
Hauled the shattered, worn and bruised Asmodeus
Back to the nethermost gaol.

So hearken,
What a fishy fume was to Asmodeus,
So is enthusiasm to inertia.
Tell me, how didst thou fare at the Garden?
What become of thine eye and hand?

Ambition: A hortative parable 'twas indeed,
But, the yarn of this unsung argonaut, will shatter
thine inner weir my Lord.
What could I say of mine lost eye and hand!
For mine unvoiced sorrow givest no words.
Behold me my Lord! I stand dejected,
Like as once lorn Hector, who stood fated,
When the potent gods utterly forsook him.
I wot not whither have mine ambitions overleapt,

that I should demerit His grace;

For vied I for the envied cornucopia,

In the glorious city of prosperity,

And like Bellerophon, onto the Aleian plains of Sorrow I fell,

That I should waste mine life in the cursed Hard Manual Labour Estate,

And to suffer such mental atrophy,

Like when by the zenith of his glory,

Sought he to scale up to touch the glittering eyes of high Uranus;

Only to incur the stings of a gad,

Bade by the wood-wroth Jove, to hurl him down.

Yea, was it not **Him, who doest wonders,** thro' all ages,

Which purloined mine whole heart,

Left me forlorn in a dry baren Isle amidst a deep of plenty!

Even now as I behold in pain, this wrecked Life-House, void of a right light and a left portal,

It killeth me; not because of the loss, or even the denied retribution;

But that failed I completely to merit His grace,

Like as once that gorgous daughter of Chelcias did.

My Lord, such accusations those villains of Manual Labour Estate hurled against an innocent me,

Like those lust drunk ancient wolves in their mating rut,

Brought against that chaste wife of Joacim. Alas! Alas the day! Alas the day my Lord!

When me at that abhorred Estate and she, **Susanna,** there at Babylon screamed out to Him, amid walking toward our scaffolds.

O her cries did rent apart His great heart,

While mine cries returned void to thumb its nose at mine oven detested visage.

But hark,

How made He haste unto her predicament, from His vaultly throne, impaling those wolves onto a Mastic

and a Holm,
And thus, exculpating the apple of His eyes.
But me, He delivered me cruelly unto mine
incriminators that they should maim the thorn of
His eye! Alas the day!
Alas the day I was born!

Will-Power: Thine woe doth lacerate the very caul of mine heart!

Ambition: Hark my Lord, seest thou me erect? Nay, Nay!
                I've long died! For beheld I, mine own life,
                Yawing away from mine cherished custody,
                As like the once king;
                Him, who was given the Excalibur,
                By Vivian, the Lady of that strange Lake,
                After bading Bedivere to return that which hath set
                him upon the Zenith of gold and glory,
                Departing sadly in a nev'r again to return voyage,
                Unto the misty vale of Avilion.
                But, till now the barge is yet to return.
                O'will it ev'r return! Will it ever!
                But reason says-never!

Auto-Suggestion: Master, time slumbereth.

Ambition: Pardon me my Lord, but I must needs to lighten this
                sore burden of mine lorn heart.
                But then, tell me my Lord, where couldst I pour
                save onto thine porous heart!

Will-Power: Do! Do it to thine heart's bent. 'Tis deep 'nough!
                Thou should'st have beheld that Great Wilderness
                of Desperation and that mountain called, Fasting.
                Hark, therein canst thou invoke divine aid when all
                things else have failed.
                His Hands surely are not shortened nor are His ears
                heavy!
                Wherefore discredit Him not my good friend,

But nevertheless, drain out thine sorrows upon mine heart.

Ambition: No longer my good Lord. I shall anchor this strayed Argosy forthwith.
I am come to seek that mysterious man, Other-Self. Know'st thou him my lord?

Will-Power: Nay my friend. In truth no one knows for sure who is he or whither be his sojourn,
Save his powers, which is too petrifying even to ponder a scintilla.
But wherefore makest thou a wilderness out of that cumbersome mystery! Fear not,
Be bold, for thou shalt go in the puissance of our aegis: For at thine disposal are these knights-Sir Imagination, Sir Wishful, Sir Five-Senses, Sir Accurate Thinking, Sir Concentration, the bold Sir Conscious, and Sir Pleasing Personality and of course, My personal guidance,
Together we'll guide and escort thee unto the great city of Prosperity.

Ambition: Thy words dryeth tears. I'll lay rest,

Chapter 7

Great Showdown

That night, Lord Will-Power threw a sumptuous banquet in Ambition's honour. Together with the fabulous knights they dined and talked things pertaining to their forth coming odyssey.

The following day the royal group including Sir Conscious escorted the argonaut out. They had not set quite far as yet from the gate when a strange figure headed towards them.

It was none other than that uncanny Mr. Failure who from afar off lifted his voice and shouted:

Failure:	Avast I say!
	Hoist your ears O ye lords!
	Hasten lightly to the gate!
	Venture not to your detriment!
	Make haste I say!
	Your adversary! Will be here anon!
Ambition:	Halt your gap thou swollen foot!
	Art thou come to pry mine life!
	Thou prattling Janus—faced traitor!
Will-Power:	Hear me thou Apple of Discord!
	Lest I rent thee asunder!
	And make a sumptuous feast of thine abhor flesh

for vultures!

Amidst the exchange the dreaded titan appeared and I waited in avidity for the earth-shaking show-down between Unemployment and the undaunted mighty heroes of the Kingdom of Within:

Unemployment: (aside to Mr. Failure) Taken by thy presence!
Nonetheless 'Tis commendable, that thou hast
prevented these numskulls.
O renegade! Clouds of Death hath engulfed thee!
Where wilt thou run! Not a power on earth,
Nor in heaven can now save thee!

Ambition: Take heed thou insolent titan!
Thou stand'st before the royal presence of the
extolled king of shining Within and his gallant
knights!

Will-Power: O abominable idiotic titan!
I've hoved! Hoved for this desired tryst!
Answer me thou gorgonic beast!
How long shall the gloomy clouds shroud the
morning star!
Take heed this day!
Thine victim a royal protégé of the kingdom!
One move even against his very hair, thou invit'st a
deadly pounce!

Unemployment: O arrogant patrician!
Before I jostle thee by the scruff of thine neck onto
the rack refine thine words!
Take heed lest thou bring'st upon thine head and
Kingdom the sword of Damocles!
For mine grievances are not arrayed against ye but
the renegade!
Turn him over and save your lives and the
kingdom!

Will-Power: Nay! Bawl out your red tales to barnacles,
Or to marines!
The spartan steel doth not bend with ease thou
foolish titan!
Wherefore I hereby cast the yoke upon cesspit and
turn over our defiance!

And Sir Conscious who was munching some nuts oppositely remarked:

Conscious: Here! (showing his nuts)
I'll turn over some peanuts!

The Rest: Ha, ha, ha!

Unemploy: Bestrew me this day, if I destroy not these and
bring to naught this puny Kingdom!

Will-Power: O foppish titan!
Gird up thine loins to greet these hornets and their
deadly stings!
Play the man not the empty cani, thou bawling cur!

The wrangle thus ended with this insolent shout and the titan went berserk with such petrifying rage, bellowing with such might as to make the welkin ring while the entire place tremored.

Fiery fumes belched from its nostrils and mouth as it rushed towards them brandishing the clubbed trident. Ambition dared not venture but the rest were as undaunted as ever and in fact seemed rather agog to greet the infernal challenge.

For in the whirling approach of tempest they began displaying such astounding fortitude; with drawn swords they too vented their spleen in leonine ferocity and charged forward like intractable bulls, yelling out the battle cries.

Lord Will-Power ran first followed by Sir Conscious and the rest;

Will-Power: Welcome to the decoy O titan!
                Terrors of Hell have yet to lay hold of mine heart!
                Who art thou O titan that I should regard!
                Cheerly, cheerly my hearts!
                Hoist ye! hoist ye!
                The banner of the majestic Within! Attack!

Conscious: Charge! Spare not an inch!
                Death to the titanic deil!

Sir Concentration: Either thine severed head or mine!

Wishful: Here I come—to dehisce thine belly!
                And garland thee with thine bowel!

Accurate: Meet this piercing basilisk O titan!
                It lusts for thee! Yaar!

Pleasing: Here I come to bury thee!
                Taste the pitchy lump O titanic Bel!

And they fell upon the titan with such indignant fury.

The battle was a short spaced bloody melee that no sooner exploded climaxed in a fearful shambles with the glorious martyr's crown, crowned upon the royal heroes and out of the utter ruins of the fabulous golden kingdom of Within, arose the immortal obelisk of glory which shall forever be worshipped as a shrine of an unyielding courage.

The hideous titanic dastard began unleashing such fearful powers, shocking strength that made their hopes of surmounting or even a pyrrhic gain to go awry; for Unemployment atrociously slew the gallant men and brought to dust the entire kingdom but captured Ambition alive.

Though slain yet by their blood laid a corner stone of their unconquerable souls. Yes my friends, though the titan cruelly slaughtered them yet failed to conquer them.

To unravel this paradox, let me at this very instant take you to that horrible, bloody battle field;

Look now! Lord Will-Power runs brandishing his greedy sword to meet the charging titan whose hoisted trident, bellowing and monstrous strides are comparable to a horrendous tornado.

Standing on tenterhooks, hearts throbbing deliriously and blood congealed by the shrilling winds of anxiety we now behold through strained eyes, the infernal titanic villain and the heroic royal gladiator in indignant groans rumbling closer and closer toward each other for a deadly embrace with each stride echoing petrifying omens!

The momentous hour any time now!

Quick, get ready for the sanguinary show-down!

They are getting closer and closer!

The hellish gates are about to break! Here it goes!

Boom!

The titan viciously swings, strikes in hammering might-the clubed thunderbolt arrows down sneeringly and the mighty king invoking the only bulwark for the hour, shields himself with his golden shield.

Oh no! The deadly comet shatters the shield, ploughs through his helmet, armour and staggers his hopes and seals the fate. The wounded King now tumbles down and rolls away with crimson blood gushing out of his head.

But hoisting his courageous banner aloft his defeat and wounds he gets up and screams:

"Under thine bludgeonings,
My head bloody, but unbowed!"

With this cry he draws a dagger and runs forward. The focus shifts now! Look-the titan's trident eye's Sir Conscious. Here it strikes! Sir Conscious shield's himself.

Oh no! the lethal blow hits bull's eye and there goes the fabulous knight sprawling on to the ground! O my!—look how the blood gushes out! O my God! No! please! Ah don't! I can't bear to watch this!

The titan raises its gargantuan right foot to flatten the wounded gladiator! Here it goes! I close my eyes! I could hear a crushing noise of the gladiator's body!

Opening my eyes—O the gruesome sight! I see a bloody spattered mess of what was once Sir Conscious and the bleeding King grappling violently with the titan; he plunges his dagger striking its rubber-like devilish skin, it bounces back to his utter shock.

The titan shrugs off and there—hammers him to death!

Unperturbed by the shocking fall of the two men, the rest in faces contorted with rage and teeth gnashing in a yearn for revenge contriving upon a means of foiling the on-slaughter, coalesced in spirits and are now encircling the titan strategically; with roots of fortitude firmly planted, poised for a head-on strafe in view of arresting its attention is Sir Accurate flanked by Sir Concentration for a simultaneous pincer thrust while the rest, Sir Wishful, Sir

Pleasing and Sir Imagination now forge a deadly phalanx to pounce from the back for the kill.

But discording their strategic embarkment, the titan turns around and faces the triune phalanx. Look! Look how the beast graphs Sir Imagination and Sir Pleasing by the neck!

By gad! Knocks them against each other with such fearful force-crushing and shattering both their helmets and heads, killing them in a trice!

While the swords struck by the two only bounced back void. Sir Accurate knuckles himself down to strike the Achilles heel, that is, titan's eyes. O no! Sir Wishful! It clubs him!

The poor gladiator now tatters. And he drops dead! The desperate Sir Accurate now strikes, but misses and the titan graps him by the neck and squeezes! O the horror! Look—the head falls off!
Now the sole remnant of this grisly carnage Sir Concentration goes berserk and charges towards his death!

Grapping him, the titan tosses up, and look!

How it batters him in mid-air itself to his death! Thus was the pathetic end of the gallant heroes.

Mr. Failure then dragging Ambition, ran a distance to shelter themselves from the oncoming dregs. Undergoing a metamorphosis concussion after the bloody massacre the titan enlarged itself, bellowed with such a might that the din of which bolted down both Mr. Failure and Ambition.

I beheld in horror in my dream, the titan going wild and wreaking havoc;—ravaging hammering down and uprooting the entire foundation of the Kingdom of Within, turning it into a rubble.

Petrified by this, Ambition espying that yonder wilderness of Desperation beyond the Kingdom's perimeter, postulating his last hope of Salvation pushed aside Mr. Failure and fled for Mt Fasting.

Pursued by the titan, collecting every iota of might, determination and faith he mounted up weary and worn and upon entering the cave of prayer exploded in hysterical outbursts of importuning screams; crying frenetically for help!

O the pathetic horror should have moved the devil's heart!

But the hideous titan Unemployment shattering the cave with its clubbed trident seized the terrified man and dashed him against a rock, breaking his armour and kicked him down.

And the frenetically screaming argonaut went tumbling down the rugged slope mutilating his body. The titan then further kicked and mauled till there was no more breath in him.

Had not Mr. Failure intervened, Unemployment would have killed him.

He was then hauled to the castle and imprisoned. Unemployment appointing a ritual execution day sealed his fate in the hands of the giant, Suicide.

But Ambition, mangled by the ignomious fiasco welcomed his execution only too gladly.

Despondence, remorse and unbearable sorrow weighed so ponderously upon him.

Chapter 8

Ambition Meets Sir Hope the Gladiator

As **Ambition** was contemplating his fated death in the hand of the giant, Suicide, in a matter of days, of his life, ventures and macabre sorrows, I beheld in my dream three people approaching him—Mr. Failure, Sir Hope a gladiator and an uncanny nymph, Precious Memories.

Together after greetings, they had elevated discourse with Ambition, endeavouring to enlighten him.

After which Sir Hope breaks open the prison gate to deliver and escort him out while Mr. Failure walks away and the nymph vanishes.

Upon seeing the argonaut, Mr. Failure breaks the silence and accosts him on the purpose of their visit:

Failure: Divine hour knocketh upon thine soul's portal,
                O argonaut, man mortal.

Ambition: O stormy Petrel! Leave thou me alone:
                The benignant alms of time from fate thrown,
                Yearn I to repose me in silent mourn
                Before the dread will of Suicide be done,
                Of hope to regain dignity I've none.
                Wherefore shall I cross the Styx anon.

I prithee O Mr. Failure—begone!

Failure: Came I to unbosom an unknown strength,
Even of Other-Self who awaits in short length.
I leave; mine patience will no longer vent.

Ambition: Alas! O mine wonderful redeemer!
Severed I the hand that reached to the mire!
In sincere repentance I now tremor,
My mentor, good Nestor, avast! O sire,
Tell me, what will thine judgment require?
O turn not thine face in indignation,
Till abase I myself as an oblation,
For the remission of mine contention.

Failure: Be thou correspondent to wisdom's thrust,
And take a dose of physic from thine past,
For upon nostalgia wilt thou be cast.

Enter now Precious memories and Sir Hope the gladiator:

Ambition: Ah! Romantic Love, lass of mine choice!

P. Memories: Touch not, for I'm not blood and flesh!
Neither am I Romantic Love but a mere shadow.
Wilt thou not then pour out thine heart's sorrows!

QUOTH AMBITION

**As I stood alone by a stormy shore, one dark mid-night,
Beholding mine shattered life, which tarried for Death with delight,
Venting such woeful tears of pain and such dire sorrows,
After being smitten by Him, who alone doeth wonders,
As I was scourged under vain hope's tantalizing shadows
And brutally mauled by grim Poverty's cruel thunders,
Mine mortal eye was suddenly ravished and drawn away;**

For I beheld an anglic ARGOSY, with flying sail.
Boarding it and flying along, I saw a golden veil;
Unveiling it, saw innocent heav'ns, like that of old tales.
And behold! There was One, in white rope, called, Ancient of Days!
Engrossed with an engineering layout, as that Book says.
He helped geometrical tools that worked upon that design.
Thus, there was born a love and adoration, never to resign.
By the cool of the lovely even-tide He now descends,

O the stifling splendours of Him, mine highest dreams transcend,
He walks in enthreal aura, so majestic—hair beard and rope,
All white, as with tears and stark sorrow I beheld in awe.
Then drew that ARGOSY, with wings like eagle but as dove;
Sailing thro' the tranquil waters of ancient Pison now,
And anchoring by the streams, I see bdillium and onxystone.
A tantalizing sight it is, of great vicarious delight.

Sitteth within mine ARGOSY, I now profoundly don
My weary cold soul held by improvisation so tight
With such sweet delectable and ecstatical pleasure.
I ponder: 't'was for whom created He Havilah's treasure?

This burning question profound, creeps upon me life ivy.
Alas in cold realization, I shed tears of envy.
Neath the bottomless pit of abject hopelessness laid I,
Yet in the hellish despondence whereof I sought to die,
Visited that strange ARGOSY, to take me to lands,
Where no man would dare go, where no populace could ever know;
To rest upon that wonderful, heavenly, the happy strands.
The Ancient of Days came walking by in glory and lo:
He unveils a misty veil by His want destroying hand,
Lo and behold! His infinite, boundless treasure I saw;
Stretching from one endless end to another endless end-
A sight staggering, astounding, I beheld by that shore.
His marvelous nature is love, compassion and goodness,
All that a man wants or ev'r longs, is there in His riches.
A mite from His treasure, canst surely brighten mine future,
Yet, left I without alms, in such agonizing torture.

Quoth I : "wherefore draweth thou me O mine soote ARGOSY
To vain fantasyI could never merit His mercy."

Answered ARGOSY: "Come away O weary Ambition,
And sail thro' the yonder misty portals of the ages,
Abode me and set aside thine dreary, sad attitude.
Haply thou mayest unlock the hidden privileges
When we survey His wondrous and marvelous miracles.

Let's fly and venture beyond the misty silvern curtain,
Maybe thou couldest discover some secret oracles!"
Flying thro;-alas, the grim fiend his evil hast attain,
Harsh and cruel seasons pitilessly came with leashing,
While sin and suffering, laden with sad turmoil came crashing!
Flying further yond, the iron curtain-an age forlorn,
Saw stanching wickedness; a society so wrecked and worn
After silvern and iron age saw I an iris arch;
Wonder edifice of His covenant's glorious art,
His immortal and immutable law it doth emblazons.
Wherefore hath He created kindly mounts and azurely tarns?
'Tis all for the delectation of mountain denizens.
His law replenisheth to overflowing the Nabob's barns,
He adorns the Levant and maketh the majestic falls,
He tendeth and stireth to productivity the soil,
He rains his blessings and presenteth the sea with atolls.
By cruels hungar's pangs, for mine only hope I did toil;
Sought I for it desperately, by the iris arch's end,
Untreasured dejection and away with an empty hand.
Unto Him sowed I a love and life so great and intense,
Which never ever did receive any recompense.
O Campanula! Defunct are the ears of populace.
Blind fools who perceive not thine sweet and comforting solace.
Wretched numskulls, tongue wielders, who hear not thine melodies.
Yet mine ears are wooed and leap, when thine knell rings!
Crabs bearing anemones knoweth not venomous tragedies,
Yet convulsed a derelict Free-crab to death by its stings.
Behold, anchored next mine ARGOSY by Great Stage Play,
By Exodus theatre beheld His miraculous drama,

Strange excitement overwhelmed, which I could not allay,
For I wept and wailed by the sting of His melodrama.
But He forsook utterly-mine woes refuseth to see.
Wherefore doth His miraculous works sore vex, trouble me?
Love I a broken reed even upon mine sad umber.
Yet mine trust in the Ancient of Days no pow'r canst sever!

Upon the height of mine sorrow,
As hopelessness pierced its arrow,
Mine ARGOSY even landed,

ON THE SHORES OF GALILEE.

Look mine ARGOSY, look yonder!
    Who's He ARGOSY, who's He that's walking!
Why's it ARGOSY, why's mine heart burning!

A barque there was, bearing some poor Arcadian wights
    Transiting yond in obedience to the master's will,

But while amid the deep, two gods came the men to kill.
    Poseidon and Boreas were they, dread were their sights.

Espying them from a far, the grisly gods then charged,
    With tidal sword and hoarse boisterous cries

As the trembling men's frighten hope flies
    And their desperate hearts in strode-light manner marched.

Amid this dastardly threat, when all hope was gone,
    When nigh the barque the bad hectors in terror rode,

Behold! the Ancient of Days was arrest abode.
    He then awaked to greet these uncouth gods and plight
    lorn

How quivered and shook the petrified gods in fear
    When they the omnipotent Ancient of Days did meet,

Thus falling prostrate at His fiery brazen feet
    When they His voice of many waters—Rhema, did hear.

    A leper once worn and waste,
    Feared to approach Him face to face.
    For he in his silly mind
    Thought, in Him favour may not find.
    Then the Saviour him rebuke,
    For such doubts with pityful look.
    And with one touch sent rolling,
    The hoary curse away, woes fleeing.

        Some fishermen by the shore
      Once by Him learnt a blesseth lore;
          Toiling till their best all spent
      They nev'r knew that infinite strength.
          But by giving empty bark
      Unto Him for use, amid plight dark,
          They were soon to reap harvests
      Beyond their efforts' best invests.
O astounded soul! What manner of man is He
Who enfeebles tempest and feedest hungry multitudes,

      Breaketh fetters and maketh whole man destitute.
Even Hades trembleswhat pow'r can it be!

How shall vanquished Sin, here shall again thrive,
    When deep in the grim shades, Death pleads for life!

Why should mortal man fear, or woes should taste,
    When Hell crawls in shame with bloody bruised face
And Fates astride ass, go mourning their fate,
    As Fear cowers and Diseases are plagued!
Say my heavenly King, Star of Wonders and Morning!

Answer! while this destitute man stands afar mourning!
Would'st thou appear before this hungry man who's afraid,
In any form other but as a bread?
Or durst thou greet this wretched, weak man who is so sick,
In any form other but as physic?
Or would'st thou meet this weary wight in thirsty fetter,
In any form other but as water?
Or see needy sumpter—that seeker of oracle,
In any form other but as a miracle?
Or would'st thou visit this guilt whipped man with sin laden,
In any form other but as gracious pardon?
Oh! Ye fortunate and envied shores of Galilee;
Bread, physic, water, miracle, pardon did see!
  'Tis mine PRAYER

Ancient of Days! For thine striking wonders,
As a destitute Man by dark stronds ponders,
    Conjures in my soul fiery gushing tears,
The billows of which scourge in east-wind sears,
    During innocence, seamy side was not,
As of wights fellowship thou freely sought.
    But wherefore came then the age of silver,
Of thine fellowship with man to sever?
A destitute Man without in groaning dies,
But no more lays He folly to his cries
    As Aurola's tears aways by morn's frown,
So are the destitute Man's pleading tears thrown.
    Yet in mine desolation's forlorn plaint,
Sought I with thine wonders to get aquaint;
    Thou didst make those lofty mounts skip like rams,
And those defying knolls like humble lambs,
    Memphian hosts led by their gods nighed the sea,
Of their ignomious doom failing to see.
    When Thou lifted up thine indignant Arm,
Their whipping defeat became Israel's psalm.
    Joshua marched in such victorious manner,
When Nissi His name became his banner,
    When His Plenty to a widow was shown,

Jirreh His holy name thus became known.
      Yet, brimming woes Thou upon me pour'st
The adamantine mirage Thou send'st
      Rages mine brief life to the edge of death,
I melt and wither by blows Thou hast dealt;
      By night Thou send'st Morpheus the horror,
To torment my soul with dreams of terror.
      By day Thou send'st Orcus the brutal,
To inflict upon me wounds immortal.

Quoth Thou; 'if thou bring'st thine offering,
I will pour out such great blessing,
      And no more room will there be to receive.'
But ever thine help I could not perceive!

ANSWERED MR. FAILURE

O the horse that swims in the deep
      And the stars by the sea-bed that creep,
All He by His great power doth keep.
      His Providence doth not sleep,
Yet complain'st thou of His goodness canst not reap.
Lift up thine eye to the heavens in lieu,
And behold Canopus the celestial flambeau!
      A question of enlightment may I ask you!
Standing upon this earthly purlieu,
      Canst thou see its glittering view.
Reckonest thou the power of chastising thy knees upon predieu?
      But unto this truth, bid thou not adieu.
O argonaut, open now the portals of thine soul
      And halt being an ignorant fool.
Thine gloomy effusions of despondence, is the thief's deadly tool,
      To impede thine clouded sight from yond hope's refulgent
      pull.
Wherefore be still and keep thine being cool

Does down-trodden, dirt smeared sapphire losses its value or
azureness?
Or, compared to turgid ones on crown any less?

Can Faun protract his powers beyond woods and grass?
To touch thine citadel, no adversities the power possess!
A great Kingdom there lieth within thee-all answers to process.

Herein is the mystery of wisdom
    And the key to the secret powers of egoism. (Gives him
    a Diamond key).
Not far from here lieth a glittering kingdom,
    'Tis called Greatwithin the source of freedom.
But 'Tis hidden to the masses and is known seldom.

Beyond Greatwithin shall arise a terrible Deliverer!
His name-Other Self, with such shocking power!
    For he and he alone thine strong tower,
At the sight of whom thine enemies shall cower,
    For he shall thine chains of misery and bondage sever.
Man was never created for poverty,
    Nor to crawl in dust in sin's severity,
Nor for failures, defeat, confusion or inferiority,
    Nor for despondence, shame, turmoil or perplexity,
But was made to walk high in royal dignity.

At the Paradise when man lost his birthright,
    When the tempter blinded his sight,
Was where sin, poverty began and swept in full might,
    Was when the barrier to THE ADONAI was sealed tight
That thou mayest not perceive THE JIREH'S light.

    O He hung upon that cruel cross!
        Tho rich, yet for thine poverty and remorse,
Became He poor and counted it all loss.
    That thou mayest have assess in full force
To His wealth and infinite source.
    Let me a heed unto thee tell.
    O, permit not that ghostly knell,
    Rung from the past bitter memories bell,
    Unto dejection and saturnine woes sell.
    For upon past's pit had many in disaster fell.

A truth from a sage I did borrow,
Recall it when tragedy aims it bow and arrow,
The simmering agonies of today's deadly sorrow,
Is the gateway to genius tomorrow
For amid sorrow, heavens the answers upon thee throw.

O, try comprehending His infinite fashion.
Reckon the pearl that comes from friction,
The oak that smiles amid erosion
And the rough road leading to high station.
Wherefore, against these adversities loose thine
tension.

To overcome the inner-man, not even can Satan,
Blind him—there'll be a Paradise Lost and Milton,
Curse him with poverty there'll be a Dicken,
Cripple his love life—there'll be a Lincoln,
Seal tight the prison gate—a Bunyan shall return.

PRECIOUS MEMORIES.

Let me now O argonaut usher thee,
Thro' the nostalgic doors of thine past,
In neither sonnet nor rhyme but in free-verse.
Hast thou not ploughed thine way thro physical puzzles,
by the tools of calculus,
or gauged the heavenly balls by pure geometry
and scaled up darkest mysteries by the light of algebra!
Hast thou not encountered the simple problems, the hard
Ones and the really tough ones!
Hadst thou not recoursed to thine mentor for positive
Solutions each time thou fail'st in the puzzle!
Even so, reckon this axiom O argonaut.
For life is but a set of mathematical problems,
Given us by that Universal Mathematical; some
Simple while others hard but some seemingly tough ones.
But there lieth a position solution to EVERY ONE of these problems.
Say argonaut! Look thou straight into mine eyes.

And declare unto me thou coward it thou possess'st any jot of courage,
That He the Heavenly Mentor had never ever once answered thee!
He hath done before and He'll do it again!
Hast He changed! As long as He remaineth the
Adonai, miracles shall not cease.
For He who once proved Himself alive after His passion
by many infallible proofs stand'th ever ready to do the same for thee.
Ephemeral Love—who awakens romantic spring in May and chastises with loneliness in winter when she departs.
Though the haunting memories of her lingers on in nostalgic
Torments, yet it shall conduct thee to the doorway to genius.
O the pouring tears from sorrow seared cheeks.
Viewed by none save the pathos filled moon.
O the tears scorned to cruel beat by Hopelessness,
Is but sleep-murdering waters to awaken that Slumbering-Giant!

QUOTH
SIR HOPE.

    Of thine state in exactitude I do perceive.
        O thine frustrations I do of my mind conceive.
    O Ambition, hark now I hereby do beseech.
        For I desire an important lesson to teach.
    Wilt thou not then came away flying upon eagle's wing!
        For a vision, stay aloft like feathered mount king.
    Even now, a myth knocketh upon mine memory.
        A fable, yet depicts thine state in atrophy.
    Even more, it shall give thee hope of deliverance.
        Doth not Tigou afar has its earthly entrance,
    Corresponding to elements of fire, water, air!
        Likewise legends doth many expounding lores share.
    Wherefore hark unto me now, tho' it may seem odd.
        As I herewith breakforth this famed fable in ode:

HERO OF MYTHOLOGICAL GENESIS

Mt.Caucasus—thou an enblem of tragedy!
Rascal Craggy Rock—why do you look so gaudy!
You good for nothing Vulture-don't be so greedy!
Even Astralea has gone blind,

And courage has dragged behind.
Villain of Olympus! Of nature so dire,

Wilt thou not of thine brutal evil retire!
Why the hell strived you to destroy the fire!

Hatred for hollow fennel stalk.
     'jealousy's thirst,' truth shall talk.

Let now the savant of the Grecian art,
Ponder solemnly at the fount of art,

That escaped the varlet's diabolical art.
And then condemn the varlet's enterprise.

For strived he thro oxen's sacrifice,
To ensnare the new-born creature of clay.

Wherefore mete out judgment without delay.
Look O look! those tears from woeful eyes,
     Now pour bitterly in unspeakable sighs.

Look O look! those creation working hands,
     Now withers away upon pitiful ends.

     Look O look! those heaven leaping feet,
     Now lay dead before Atrophy's cruel seat.

Titan! Star and Hero of mythological genesis

Now so wretched and worn—what fate it is!

O, hope forlorn and whipping agonies like octopus's ink.

Fetters thine only meat and throes thine drink.
Yet in silent endurance for man's sake gladly dost thou bear.
Remember titan, Dr. Time doth care.
     'Say Dr. Time! Thine chariot is too slow,
And you have thirty thousand miles to go.
     Who is to try the mettle of the cruel chain?

For the good titan lieth in macabre pain.'
     Say Man! Just look now, who is behind me.

Him whom I'm carrying now, can't you see?
     Who cometh to turn a captivity;

To break the triad sisters' evil proclivity,
     Roast the greedy vulture to set a feast,

And thro' Mt. Caucasus divert the lethe.
     'Hello mister Heracles, how do you do!'
     Okay mister okay same to you too.

Chapter 9

Rescue of Mr. Diffidence & Showdown Between Sir Hope & Giant Suicide

With these words Sir Hope breaks open the prison gate while Precious Memories vanishes and Mr. Failure walks away. Thus Sir Hope led Ambition out of the castle, and they headed for that strange Kingdom-Great Within by way of a thick forest maze.

The manacle of quandary was thus snapped by the riveting wonders of that mysterious man, the invincible Other-Self. Trudging out of the forest maze they encountered that giant, Suicide, who was about to slay and devour a poor victim named Mr. Diffidence. In a terrible duel that ensued, Sir Hope slew the giant, rescuing the victim and then went on. As they headed:

Diffidence: Say! What manner of man art thou Sir Hope,
                Whose baffling, sparing finesse pushed nether the
                vexing star of mine devourer?

Hope: Marvel not at this, I am but the least of the gallant
                conductors who await thee, in the Kingdom of Great
                Within.

Diffidence: Mean'st thou there are other valiants, Sir Hope,
                besides thee?

Hope: Yea, good friend! Providence hath stored for thee, as bountifully as the spangled heavens,
Shining wonders as crystal Capella,
I say to thee, when we get there onon,
Surprises shall blind and gorge distance, between the beholding and apprehending.
Tell us good friend, how camest thou hither,
What goaded thee to betake this odyssey?

Diffidence: T'was by sowing and watering of sundry yarns, of those who hath ventured successfully from abhorred Penury,
Whose life vein rich, fed mine wish,
Till it grew to be an oak.
But alas, to withdraw only hither;
For this sultry ground being rather hostile   to roots of Rubicon.
Like as when, the Lagartos, the great ugly Lizard,
Sneaks behind Sir Walter Raliegh's galley by stealth,
While the expedition fares on, to prey upon the unwary moor-boy,
Who hath unboated for a cool fresh plunge;
Suddenly, shock and fear seizes their hearts,
Feelings of regret sweep and courage sinks,
When the Largartos devoureth the boy.
Venturing by taking the lane of illhealth,
Stumbled I into a mire ere ferreted by that hideous giant, the dreadful Suicide.
Harken Sirs, slain was I a megatime ere the cruel Molach of anxiety,
Until ye my dear friends exorcised these tormenting demons.

Ambition: Friend, hast thou not met that wonderful man, Mr. Think Rich?

Diffidence: Nay sir.

Ambition: How is it my friend that thou didst venture, without
              a guide or at least an armour?
              Hast thou not heard the perils?

Diffidence: Whether there be perils or great dangers or for the
              want of aegis I wist not,
              Nor didst anyone or heavenly being guide me,
              Nor a Veronica whilst for Golgotha.
              Had I but known of these snares and disasters,
              Ah! An obstinate mule would I have been,
              To even dream of such a venture as this;
              Like as once in covetous obedience, to King Balak's
              regal conjuration, to pronounce malediction upon
              Israel,
              Balaam, who hied from Pethor post to Moab,
              That sacrilegious generation, issued from the
              incestuous union by a cave afar Zoar,
              For sacred dialogue with the potentate,
              Who sought a port in the impending storm,
              Was interposed by a sword wielding prince, bidding
              his wise talking ass to stay still,
              Which obdurately refuseth a step more.
              Even now 'Tis the cords of ye both, that bind and pull.
              Now dear friends, are we not going unto the city of
              Prosperity?

Hope: Yea friend.

Diffidence: Then, why the need to enter this Kingdom,
              Which thou call'st Great-Within?

Ambition: 'Tis to seek that one man, who alone canst conduct
              us to Prosperity.
              His name, Mr. Other-Self! He alone my banner!
              And he will ensnare every dread peril;
              For outwitted Disaster shall entrap itself,
              As like once when the Elohim Nissi,
              Led the pastoral Semitic people from Succoth thro'

the littoral Sinai,
Rameses JR and his imperious cavalry,
Pursuing in impetuous insanity,
Hoisted their own petard ignomiously, in the parted
Sedge,
Whilst the Memphian gods, which led them by mid-
air, stood aghast,
Cowering helplessly as they beheld their ardent
worshipers' floating corpses,
Broken wheels and carcasses of horses;
Not even their River King, Petesuchos,
Durst go unto their rescue for great fear.
Or that magic wielder, Peter Magus;
Sorcerer and incarnated satan,
Who was relieved of both powers and life by the holy
apostles, Peter and Paul.
Or 'Tis like as that mortal Judge of clay,
Who durst once try that Great Immortal Judge;
Him did alas, fell upon divine judgment,
Scorned by his own wife Procla,
As she saw the angel flying off with his severed head.

Diffidence: What is he?

Ambition: You Sir Hope, what is he?

Hope: Pardon me my friends. In truth I say this-
              Even I wot not who or what is he,
              Though he exists somewhere at our Kingdom;
              Like the mystery that warps upon Orion's death,
              What goaded him to kick the bucket?
              Scorpio ar Diana?
              Haply my Lord,
              King of Great-Within, his highness Lord Ego,
              Could unravel this mystery.
              And in fact,
              The King heard about thine great predicament,
              And hastened me and Sir Position Emotion unto

thine aid.
But due to some commitments, I know not what, Sir
Positive has delayed.

Ambition: Thou hast made me a debtor!

Diffidence: But Sir Hope, me-seems thou art sufficient.
For with winkless eyes watched I the display of thine
strength;
Wherefore thou canst conduct us.
For thy presence an Amazon Girdle,
Wherefore dare I vouch to fight alongside thee.
Let's not entangle ourselves with that mystery and
gamble away time.

Ambition: Prattle not, thou callow.
Thou art beguiling thy self with Ai.

Hope: He is right my friend, the source am I not.
You have yet to behold the fearful powers, of those
titanic hosts.
Nor could'st the powers, of mine entire Kingdom so
multiplied, a megatime, match the evil domain,
Save that mysterious man, our only guide;
For he shall guide thee thither wondrously,
Like the bright and morning Venus,
Which once led the triad Magi from Babylonia,
Unto the little town of famed Ephrath;
Them who brought gifts of shinning ornament, tree
and scrub resins to adore the Prince,
Who left His glories above to abode amongst earthly
destitute men and sinners;
To mend broken-hearts of the down-trodden and to
cheer-up poor ostracized plebeians.

Diffidence: If this be so, then lead us to thine stay.
Now Sir, desirous am I to know in depths the city of
Prosperity.

Hope: The city of Prosperity is a land of Plenty watered by
four sweet rivers,
With gardens, meads, founts and countless delight,
Where hunger, want, privation, fears, inferiority,
remorse, anxieties, tears, rags, huts, torments will
not be found.
Yet, more than just material, but also spiritual
wealth that suffices the wholeman;
With harmony, tranquility, success, happiness and
a good sound mind.
Whereunto are forbidden knaves, swindlers and the
corrupt;
For these are welcomed but, at another city, nigh
Prosperity, called—City of Mammon.
Mammon though rich yes, in material plenty, but is
void, of the tree of life.
Even once besought, at the wilderness of Tekoa in
Judaea,
That Old Nick, to allure into Mammon,
The omnipotent Savior of Mankind.
But him, was brutally cut and wounded by the
double-edges sword,
And he fled cackling back to Hell in sore pain and
shame.
Mammon is watered by the roots of evil,
Wherefore the ones there fall upon diverse perversion
and lust,
Unlike the matured ones, at the good city of Prosperity.
Objective of wealth therein at Mammon,
Is to fan their selfish, gorgonic lusts;
(which is the very seed of destruction);
As like in amorous trance, the randy, wealthy
Playboy of Olympus,
Who once made unto the ancient land of Argos,
(Thence a dominion of King Acrisius)
Bearing a bouquet of gold to seduce the ruler's
disfavoured daughter, Danae who was immured
within the tower of Brass.

Ambition:	By this I suppose that Mammon city, Is no better than Penury.
Hope:	Yea. It is also a place of torment.
	For material wealth could'st never bring true wealth.
	But it is indeed regrettable to say, that the mystical Kingdom of Within did not heed this truth;
	For hath they conducted, yea many, unto this perverted city,
	Safe our Great Kingdom, for we always warn argonauts of Mammon and its evils.
	Whereas the city of Prosperity, is roundness in value;
	Therein wilt thou prosper in spirit, soul and body.
Diffidence:	'Tis exciting, I can't wait to get there!
	Ambition! wherefore let melancholy frump thine vein?
	Wilt thou not cheer up!
Ambition:	Nay friend. I await that man, who alone can lift up this fuchsia visage cipher.
	Betwixt fugacious hour and expectation anxiety doth enjoys sore fulsomely.
	This sad droop could'st be hoisted by no cheer, comfort nor charismatic quickening
	Save, the healing touch of him—the mysterious man.
	By him shall mine nights be inflamed with lights;
	Like as those flickering lights on hillocks,
	During Fiesta of that La Bonne Lady, Sainte Anne, at theFoot of the Big Hill,
	In the exotic Aurea Chersonesse,
	Seen once by this lorn poet, whereto made he,
	In sore desperation as a pisaller,
	To disentangle his imbroglio,
	And to escape macabre indigence,

When piqued by tales strange so wonderful,
Of those thronging masses in gratitude,
For divine deliverance from hopeless wants,
And healed of incurable diseases,
Wherefore jubiliant joys make pilgrimage,
To fulfill their vows thro' pennant begging,
Lighting—up of candles and offertory to the white
Lady,
By whose great blessings, those bold, early mission
palmers from France,
Came sailing to the afar Eastern stronds,
Armed with immortal weapon—the Holy Cross.
Alas! nor the Father nor the Spirit,
Nor the Son nor his mother nor Grand Anne,
Would ever relieve woes of this destitute man;
Nor see his plight nor hear his opportunings.
Or shall I with this measure of faith,
Append wings and fly unto Siloa's brook,
And lament unto thee O Great Father!
Could Goshen be the place, to vent mine pleads-
To move thine great Hand of deliverance?
Is Carmel the mount, mine reproach shall cease?
Or shall I travail after thee, O son,
And drag this dead life by Tiberias stronds,
To win thine compassion and miraculous touch!
From whence could I conjure from thine mouth
Those tempest calming words unto mine life!

Hope: Toss it away, O Ambition, I know, thou bemourn'st
the loss of thy eye and hand.
Let a spider tutor thee O argonaut;
Though losses it a leg amid grappling, with a
poisonous prey, doth its loss persist?
Nay! It groweth again!
Ev'n so, thine loss, is not perennial.
Wherefore be of good cheer.
We shall anon enter sweet paradise,
And thou shalt behold trees hung with jewels,

And seek immortal leaves like once Gilgamesh,
Who visited Water-Encompassed-Eden.

Diffidence: O argonaut, be thou not antagonistic, to divine ways.
For thus saith the apostle, that all things worketh together for thine good.
Harken unto me—perhaps there's some good in the loss of thy eye, arm and sufferings.
Wherefore be receptive to the admonishes of Epictetus—
Whereby alter not, that which thou art powerless to do so,
But rather exhibit indifference, so as to drown the powers of sorrow.
Now let me show thee wherein is freedom:
There has to be first, recognition in the existence of predestination,
This recognition leadeth to sang froid and harmonisation of thine will to it,
Thereby freeing, making thee virtuous.

Ambition: Friend, thou hast fallaciously allied thyself with Zeno by Stoa.
O but I wish, mine understandings perceive not the delusions of such reasoning that it may be a salve.
Say'st thou, that freedom is by virtue of recognition and stark submission to predestination!
If this be sound, then, t'will not be possible to alter our lives, nor characters nor situations.
Can a man be truly free by being chained, irrevocably to predestination!
Wherefore then the need for the gift of will, which the good Creator hath bestowed upon man!
Did not Zeno assert that virtuousness or evil resides in the exercise, of the will itself!
Wherefore me-seems, there is a rancid in this reasoning-
For man is both free and bound, 'Tis absurd.

'Tis indeed a common knowledge that man, by
wielding his will-power hast altered, many a character
and situation,
Thus, doing away with all predestination.
And more over, it is not possible in every circumstances
to put on an indifferent attitude always,
Especially when we saw thy sore plight in the hands
of that giant, Suicide.

Hope: Thou hast indeed spoken right O argonaut,
Yet many a time, my friend, dost thou swoon, in thine
positiveness.
Be warned therefore, of thine attitude, both of thine
thinking and confession.
Heed negativism, as thou would'st heed that deadly
gorge-Messina;
Imposed betwixt Italy and Sicily,
That whirls sneeringly with brutal terror,
That towers grisly with shocking horror;
The eerie ambience, hovering the ghostly deep,
Is stormed whole day and night perpetually, with
congealing winds and hoarse, boisterous waves;
Making their diabolical abode there, on either side
of this simmering strait, to pry upon poor unwary
sailors,
Are two heinous monsters—abominable queens!
On the left, crouching neath a burnished Clift,
Under the doleful deep, mystically hid,
Is that sea-dragon—hideous **Charybdis,**
Who sucks on the blue waters thrice a day,
Engendering such a baneful vortex,
Wherein have sunk, channeling to its belly,
Many a ship full of men—all victims;
At times, not withstanding her ferocity,
She even challenges the Almighty to a fight,
Scorning him from her watery throne,
By spouting out water high up to sky.
Next, on the right, within a stygian cavern, of a craggy

Clift,
Abodes that goddess, Petrifying **Scylla**—unspeakable
horror!
Above her hips (begird with green sea-hounds-
Wolvish pups, wielding cerberian ferocity)
A gorgonic feminine form, with serpent locks,
And below, shark's body covered with rind,
Pronged by scorpionic tails with immortal stings,
That ceaselessly swish in snaky rattles.
From her ghastly lair, so dank and fiendish,
She and her growling curs in ravenous rage,
Descry sea-frontiers for any sailors,
To satiate their murderous jaws with blood.
O Ambition, thy life, 'Tis unstable;
As like hills at Cape Fara which uncrown their tops,
During the disequilibrium of the premonitory,
Wwhen the weird sage, Archimedes,
Poles this Earth-Barge thro' choppy parts, of our
celestial deep neath Zodiac's cope,
That over-arch's her gliding pathway above.

Chapter 10

Showdown between Sir Hope and Monster Unemployment

While they spoke, while walking along an elevated, narrow pathway where an either side were steep ravines, suddenly that dreaded governor, Unemployment came in front:

Ambition: O dreaded titan, leave us in peace!

Unemployment: I'll leave with a Carthaginian peace!

Ambition: O fiery Nemesis, wherefore pursue thou me
                So relentlessly?

Unemployment: Harken thou fool; thy fate and destiny Is ignomiously fixed and no power canst alter thine baneful course!

Ambition: Nay, to pursue me thou'll never catch up!
                Harken, hast thou not reckoned the paradox of Zeno of Elea, O thou vain Achilles!
                For to catch up this tortoise, thou'll nev'r!

Unemployment: You freakish, one-eyed pariah! Durst thou vie in metaphysics, you gibbering Zenoist!
                I'll doctor over and make thee swallow thine dislocated shoulder!

Hear this block-head;
I'll never yield mine purpose!
Now, return forthwith to Hard Manual Labour Estate
while the sea is still calm.

Hope: Yea, certainly thou would'st not now, titan.
Take heed! I know thou could'st destroy us all with
just one dread blow with thine mighty fist;
For such are thine fearful powers and might which
we are cognizant.
But bewarned;
For there lieth somewhere, in that cosmic deep,
Yond the glittering Kingdom of Great-within,
A MAN! In a mysterious slumber, whose name,
spelleth thine destruction.
His name is called, the invincible Other-Self!
To him shalt thou yield as when in latter days, Death
and grim Hell, disgorge their living dead, yielding
before the Ancient of Days.

Unemployment: Even if his existence a reality,
Yet will he succumb to this strong trident of mine.
If haply he matches me, then, I swear by that solemn
river that he can never, never, never, match even a
tenth, of the powers of Lord Poverty,
Nor that mighty, omnipotent god, Fate.
Now, yield amicably or greet death!

Ambition: Behold now, a wilted man O titan!
As in Troy's embering hour when Poseidon began
spreading irefully his dreadful quakes,
Hateful Juno garroting the populace with her flaming
hands,
Revengeful Minerva, fuming her stormy clouds
And wrathful Jove gathering the reins of the Grecian
army to hoof over,
Aeneas resolutely resolved to with stand the on-
slaughter to the end,

A resolve which sank not into oblivion,
But bore a seed to bring the Golden Age to Latium,
Here I stand before thee as like wounded lamb before
a ravenous wolf.
Yet I will not flee nor yield unto thee;
Already thou hast taken, O grim titan,
The gilt of mine gingerbread when cast upon Hard
Manual Labour Estate.
Wherefore I no longer dither before Death nor thee.
And this mine resolve; mine portals are sealed unto
thine voice as like that Eastern Gate,
Thro' which even once the Lord of Host passed thro'.
As in the allegory of the cave by Socrates;
Can the enlightened man, who hath seen light, yea
glorious light of heav'ns,
Return nether and be happy? Nay, nay!
Rather than returning I'm persuaded,
Yea so utmost, to battle thee to death.
By the mysteries that link the mind and body,
Even the subjective and the objective,
(Of which that Cartesian theorist disputed
erroneously the existence of the element of extension
or geometrical properties in the subjective realm,
But did throw up his hands in despair before the
royal lass Of Palatinate),
My positiveness shall triumph over thee!

Diffidence: Take heed titan, lest we set thee upon
Ducking stool and dip the garrulity out
Of you!
(To Sir Hope) Fear not Sir Hope, I'll stand hind thee
and fight!

And when the titan belched out its thunderous fury at this
insolent retort, poor Diffidence fearfully shrieked in shock and fled
for his life.

But alas, tripped over a stone, plunging down to his ghastly death into the ravine. Sir Hope than drawing out his sword fell upon Unemployment with utmost might but just as expected the titan slew the valiant gladiator with one blow after which grapping hold of Ambition by the neck, spoke thus, "My desires forbid that thou should'st taste an instant death. Only a lingering, tormenting death would gratify me."

The bellowing titan then in a raucous laughter plunged into the argonant's belly and sides its fearful dagger, fatally mutilating him and then threw him down the ravine. Thus Ambition went tumbling down screaming in a trail of blood. After this the titan walked away.

Chapter 11

The kingdom of GreatWithin

Fighting then for his moribund life in the shocking face of the gushing blood from his nose, mouth and fatal wounds, he staggered pass in agonizing groans through the scrub, rocky pathway a distance and then collapsed. Faintly removing his golden ring, he uttered, "My determinations forbid that I should die before beholding my redeemer, the mysterious man, and the invincible Mr. Other-Self."

Upon casting the ring, Auto appeared, who then seeing his blood drenched master stood dumbfound. Following the instructions, Auto helped him up; through great difficulty clambered up the ravine and arrived at a knoll called Idea.

Embittered by the unabated harasses of Unemployment and the tantalizing fancies of the city of Prosperity, nothing could have sustained him except for the riveting thoughts of the mysterious man, the invincible Mr. Other-Self who now lays in a mysterious slumber beyond the kingdom of GreatWithin, who and who alone could avenge his sufferings.

Auto soon discerning the knoll's mysterious linkage to the Kingdom of GreatWithin plunged his sword onto the knoll. Suddenly the hill parted into two and below there was a turbulent lake with a fearful vortex, whirling amid spouting reddish fumes.

Auto then grapping tight Ambition, together plunged into the lake's vortex and they were then immediately absorbed and transported down in a lightning speed.

Suddenly they were cast upon a glittering ground and lo and behold, before their thunderstruck eyes was an irisdescent kingdom; adorned with precious gems, diamonds sapphires, garnets and pearls. This was more than I could take in my dream, for I was totally paralyzed by its breathtaking splendour!

The dumbfound Ambition produced that diamond key from his bosom, staggered towards the glittering gate and unlocked it. Auto then flung wide the gates. And just then Sir Positive from afar off saw the weary men and rushed to greet them.

But Ambition collapsed in pain and was taken to the kingdom's physician, Dr.Time, a centaur, at a magnificent palace. He then began treating him with strange herbs.

After several days in a coma Ambition began recovering. When he regained his consciousness:

Ambition: How came I hither,
              What hath ravished me from that sultry ambience
              of dark sorrow, wherein was I even a while ago unto
              this ethereal faerie land?

Dr.Time: 'Tis in concordance with purpose divine,
              Hath thou stumbled upon this citadel by way of
              sorrow's mysterious pathway.
              Thou hast fared well in thine determination.

Ambition: Sir, while wending our way hither, Sir Hope
              and I ran afoul with that adversary, abominable
              Unemployment,
              Which slew the conductor who lifted me from grave;
              Like as once Zeus, who slew Apollo's son, Aesculapius,

Who by the health serpent hath raised many a dead to glorious life,
Thereby incuring the wrath of Hell's King.
And me, by its hideous bodkin did bore, alack, into mine vitals dire gorges,
Bringing to naught, hope's last glow.
Me—thought then, not even centaur Chiron could'st have worked healing upon mine fatal wounds so deep;
Whereupon engendered such gruesome pain, from the ravine till expired I hither,
Whose torment bulls gored me in periodic charges,
Like the seething entrails of Old Faithful, spouted forth in intermittent vomits.
Yet strange is thine physic that hast made me whole.

Dr. Time: Behold argonaut, the healing physic that hath made thee whole is of thine own choice.

Ambition: What mean'st thou by this?

Dr. Time: Hark now prithee. Thine eye hath not given this truth its due recognition,
And yet unknowingly was there born within thee, this tenet,
Even the proper budget, of the hours given thee;
By worthy indulgence in self-culture hast thou added strength upon strength,
And paved way for mine healings.
But must I warn thee in truth, for thine wounds are not every wit whole.
O that titan, hath so inflicted such immortal wounds, beyond compare,
Which hast even defied mine skilled hands.

Ambition: Alas! Have I given chase to vain rainbow,
And untreasured a forlorn pot of hope.
But Sir, tell me, what about mine eye and arm?

Art thou not able to create anew?

Dr. Time: No son, mine powers are powerless in these matters.
Me-seems thine wretched fall is indeed horrendous!

Ambition: In like manner fell I, weltering down from the ethereal
skies;
Slipped ov'r board by folly, from mine winged Argo
unto fated doom.
Nor was mine fall, and mine desperate screams
unseen or unheard by all these three worlds.
Yet wherefore should I encumber mineself, with the
Stygian's or Visible realm's insouciance.
But 'Tis the Empyrean's hostility, that sore shattereth
me;
For that great Right-Hand which once lifted the
drowning rock out from the tempest tossed waters
in the blue Deep of Chinnereth,
Forsook me, stood away, with His omnipotent arms
obdurately folded,
And the omniscient ears which once heard the cries
of an unstrung old blind man by Jericho's highway,
sealed against my vents:
As like fair Helle, who once whilst fleeing the Boeotian
region,
Astride pillion the aurea fleeced, winged ram, in
transit to the far off Colchis, dismounted down;
Like a mortal flower's tumbling descend,
When cast from the ethereal skies she dropped;
Wafting down screaming, thro the glittering dusts of
Iris she descended,
Further down to sink pass warbling larks amidst
their long mid-air fly,
Then rolling down lower clime, to suffer rebuff from
wonton winds,
And before the tir'd vermilion expanse
Of the gloaming, before the potent, but,
Indifferent gods of Olympus, she alas,

Fell screaming down to utter perdition;
Whose sable grave whereupon became known
As Hellespont in the Aegean realm.

Dr. Time: Fear not, away with thine plaint! Be of good cheer!
Tho' there exists a bourn for mine healing virtues,
Yet there's one, the strange sleeping one, whose pow'rs unbounded;
Liken to Jehovah Rapha's Infinite powers;
Behold he shall arise, out of the stark, mighty bottomless depths of the cosmic deep,
Lurked neath dimensions, so metaphysical,
Of which no man knoweth, or canst comprehend,
To heal thee every wit whole.
But yea, not only heal so completely, but shall also remove every scar, restoring thy eye and limb.
His name is so terrible, his name spelleth death to impossibilities,
His feared name being—the invincible man, Mr. Other-Self!

Ambition: Yea many wert the times, whereby I almost persuadeth me to part from mine main purpose to devote mine endeavours to seek and know in depths this strange man.
T'will be no fool's errand to do so, yet do I faint in this maze.
        Prithee Sir open unto me this riddle,
For I canst not rest me well till know I who the mysterious man, Other-Self is.

Dr. Time: Son, the truth is no one knoweth who that man, Other-Self is!
Lord Ego, shall be able to help thee in this matter.

    Dr. Time then had Auto and Ambition ushered into the kingdom's glittering palace to meet the King, Lord Ego where they were given such a royal welcome.

That night the King hosted the hero and Auto to a big banquet along with his fabulous knights:

Lord Ego: My men!
               Unto him who hath fallen upon the secret of the ages—this haven, be the Bacchanian crown be vested.
               Bully for you, O argonaut! Cheerly then!
               Rejoice exceedingly!
               The evil star of thine adversary shall set anon!

Ambition: My Sire, the strangeness of thine kingdom, doth confound me.
               Prithee, expound in height, depth and in width the plan and good purpose of its existence.

Lord Ego: What! Has it not entered thine good knowledge, the truth of thine heritage;
               That thou art an heir to this paradise!
               For this reason hath the Creator hath founded this kingdom;
               Tis is to reprieve and aid argonauts like thee.
               These fabulous knights thou seest,
               Are but thy servitors by divine hest.
               They shall be thine conductors,
               To guide thee to that city of Prosperity.

Ambition: Verily say I unto you, that thy words indeed shock'st me like a Leviathan that couldst live amongst homo sapians in baren land;
               Or the viviparous Humpbacks a frisking by Hawaian seas;
               Wherein sea-hunters neath its billows to explore— sandy beds,
               Are wonder struck by the whalely cadence,
               Of gentle singing leviathans aplay,
               Whereunto have they come from feeding havens in

Bering sea coasts or coves of Alaska.
For it maketh this wretched destitute man to one of high-born.
Yet will I in nowise transgress my bounded-duty,
For I shalt not entertain any treacherous thought
of accepting thine gracious providence.

Lord Ego: What! Wilt thou not then make known the reason for making a mockery to disgrace thine divine inheritance?

Ambition: Prithee, let patience rule thy benign judicial heart;
It is not a mockery I intend,
But that should fate await, then, let me be its sole target.
Even now as I speak, the dread, bitter memories of the ruins of that Golden Kingdom, called Within, doth rankle and strike mine heart,
For mine trail to that land, waxed a Trojan horse,
By which entered that dastard, grim governor of Sorrow,
Thus confounding the bulwark of their aegis,
Brutally slaying those men-gallant conductors and the mighty king, Lord Will-Power.
Therewithal became the shining Kingdom, like what became once of Olympian Tyrus.
O that I be my judge, would I reckon hanging be thus too kind for a traitor like me.
O mine tears flood.
Bold they were, fabulous was the Kingdom;
Rare, precious, so peculiar—thus Within.
But that ravenous beast, demised them entirely;
Like as the ferret cat which makes inroad upon the noisy scrub-bird,
Clawing apart the pitchy song-bird,
Whose rare beauty goads the ornithologist, to gravitate towards its habitat nigh Perth's forest,
With bi-optic glass, to view and study the near-flightless bird of West Australia.

Lord Ego:	Now, wherefore open'st thine hind-sight portal to the striking Bolide of past!
	Prithee, laden not, but put a hermetic seal.
	Hark, know you not that there will not be found any halcyon pathway in thy progress,
	Or if being fettered to lachrymal chains,
	Thou canst keep the meridian out of reach!
	Wherefore then, drown'st thou upon the turbulent lachrymose and keep'st out the sunshine!
	To assuage thine pain, must I needs to open this strange truth:
	For the Kingdom of Within is puny compared to ours and ought not be leaned upon wholly.
	Is it not written,
	Lean not upon thine own understanding.
	Those bold but presumptuous men's pow'rs are limited.
	Hark, but thou canst draw upon this kingdom unbounded powers and great strength by reason of its link to the seventh heavens.
Ambition:	If ought not be depended upon wholely,
	Why doth it fall neath the Creator's handiwork,
	And hence His purpose?
Lord Ego:	Tis to aid thee in basic intelligence and knowledge that may'st solve light problems,
	But when impossibilities loom before thee,
	Then should'st thou recourse to this bijou land,
	To draw upon its infinite intelligence and wisdom.
Ambition:	Thou hast indeed enlighteneth me in this matter my lord,
	But still must I needs to know if thine conductors can match that hideous governor of Sorrow.
Lord Ego:	If we run afoul him, we shall be crushed.
	This must thou needs to hold before thine mind;

For there await in thy odyssey, titans, mightier than hideous Unemployment himself.

To quote a few, there is that titan Fate, grim god of that kingdom called Superstition,

Great titan Ignorance, and above all the mighty Lord Poverty, the greatest and mightiest of the entire titanic hosts.

Besides corporeal titans thou hast to face,

There are also incorporeal demonic beings, of spirit world which thou hast to battle.

In truth, the combined strength of these conductors,

Are like dust to one of these evil titans.

Against these formidable adversaries,

We can only but confront with No-Man,

Our weapon to balance the tilted scale.

Ambition:	O, heaven's nest been fouled!

Isn't there a man or a valiant to challenge these titans!

O how cowardly is it to evade or sneak pass.

Isn't there a valiant to crush these titans?

Knights:	Yea, there's one!

Lord Ego:	Yea, there is one!

That great mysterious one!

To think of him and his terrible powers,

Maketh my hair rise and bones to tremble!

For he is like a ferocious lion.

The entire titanic and demonic host,

Are like a feeble lamb before this lion;

For such are the horrifying powers of him—the Invincible Man, Other-Self!

Oh! Why did the Creator ev'r bestow such frightening pow'rs and horrifying might upon him I wist not.

He now lieth in a deep, deep, deep slumber, somewhere in the cosmic dimensions.

Ambition:	Who is he and whither could I seek him?

For as a drowning man sore struggles for life,
I now struggle to seek him.

Lord Ego: The truth is, no one wots who this strange man or
             being is! But yet, there mayest be a way:
             There lieth an oracle not far from here at the cosmic
             island.
             Therein dwelleth an amazing, but a crazy giant,
             Who by reason of the greatness of might and powers
             have been greatly mistaken for the mysterious man
             by many wights;
             Who is all knowing yet knoweth nothing,
             All powerful yet timid,
             Infinitely wise, yet so foolish.
             Hark, for there is no mystery which he would not
             unfold,
             Nor any task he could not perform.
             The giant's name—Sub-Conscious.

Ambition: May the Ancient of Days dilt thee richly for thy loving
             kindness.
             Now, no longer does it meet that I should further
             remain Time's prodigal son,
             For must I make haste forthwith to this oracle and
             seek the giant—Sub-conscious.

Lord Ego: Wilt thou not stifle thine haste, my good friend!
             Cry thou not for the moon without a price!

Ambition: What! Say'st thou 'Tis an impossible task to meet
             the giant?

Lord Ego: Yea.

Ambition: Tell me then my Lord; what then be the price?
             Am I a maneless lion to fear death!
             Nay, verily, verily say this argonaut;
             For gladly will I throw mine life as sop to Cerberus
             And bear the sore burden of Atlas a thousand year

to possess the knowledge of who and what is that
man—the mysterious Other-Self be,
And to know of his terrible powers and might.

Lord Ego: The price thou hast to pay is to invoke the oracle to
                set at liberty the crazy giant,
                Now bound so helplessly by evil spells.
                Hoist thine ears; on sundry occasions of yore,
                Hath a number of spirits from Poverty, floundered
                to infringe our land,
                But of late, one named Negative Emotion,
                Whose horrors transcending dread Mephistopheles
                himself, succeeded so subtlety.
                By its art, hath this demon cut asunder the virtues
                of the good giant, turning him to a fiendish,
                unmitigated beast,
                Whose ferociousness can be conceived like that of
                the old dragon,
                Who by its madness and rage in end times,
                Shall draw a third part of the stars of heav'n by its
                tail.

Ambition: By gad! How then now? Is he on loose?

Lord Ego: Fear not, our kingdom is now sealed and he nor the
                demon can now penetrate hither.
                But within which space, albeit a short one,
                No tongue could describe the great may-hem
                wreaked upon our Kingdom by that crazy giant;
                T'was indeed a herculean task for my men and
                I, especially Sir Self-Discipline and Sir Positive
                Emotion to battle.
                Wherefore then, let my counsel rule thee to the
                letters,
                When thou goest there by the closing of sun morrow,
                Take with thee Sir Self-Discipline and Sir Positive
                Emotion;
                Forthwith set for the island.

By all cost avoid a confrontation with the wild giant.
But head for the abominable temple, called Negative
Confession,
Wherein dwelleth the demon, guarding a fetish idol
called Negative Influence.
A strange idol indeed;
For it exerteth spells upon the good giant.
Thus the demon maintaineth control over the giant
by dint of this idol.
Hark now;
To enfranchise the giant, must thou needs to destroy
the evil temple, the idol and the demon itself.

Ambition: Truly thou art an anise and thine words an aniseed.
For the sweet flavouring of hope, hath removed the
very vapours of mine life.
Let us wherefore plunge in wassail and exult in
this propitious hour before answering duty's call
morrow!

Chapter 12

Raiders of the Temple of Abomination

The following night the four men headed towards the isle with Sir Discipline ferrying the boat, Sir Positive Emotion standing afore with left arm akimbo and right hand shading his descrying eyes while Ambition and Auto sat together.

As they drew nearer and nearer the eerie island, the giant's homeric laughters, bellows, shrieking groans, swelled and overwhelmed the stillness. But emboldened by the mutual presence they headed undaunted landing upon the cloistered foggy island of stygian forest mazes and mountains with their mission firmly rooted.

Taking cognizance of the dire consequences should they run afoul the crazy giant they made their way surreptitiously through the gloomy forest mazes in trail of the abominable temple. The foreboding of a strange full moon which lighted the path, spelling terrors of howling werewolves, prompted Sir Positive Emotion to forewarn them of a sinister linkage of it to the demonic activity on its full swing on the island.

On espying the temple afar off they halted to descry before venturing on to reconnoiter the simmering ground.

Nearing its vicinity, a vivid sight of satanic horror greeted them; the shrine housed a Lucifer's statue which seemingly vibrated with life in that its ugly protracted eyes was emitting reddish beams. But the demon was no where found:

Ambition: Hearts!
             Play the lion and set aflame the Thames,
             By hoisting the banner in this conflict!
             The success giveth the open sesame,
             To the mysteries of Mr. Other-Self.
             The momentous hour has come.
             Sir Positive, Auto, harken ye then,
             The endowed finesse of ye in dealing with incorporeal
             beings,
             Very well befit that ye both should greet the
             Mephistophelian varlet while . . .

Auto: But lo, the demon is not.

Ambition: But nevertheless tarry ye without, employing your
             eyes as vigilant night-watch,
             Nimbleness sharper than double edges sword,
             While Discipline and I, chosen Levites,
             Shall enter within the evil sanctuary,
             To offer the pious ramrod oblation to the horrid
             statue of perdition.
             Hark, while remaineth there a meagre time,
             Let us then gird up our loins and arm us to the hilt
             lest we fall for its wiles.
             For once begineth the deadly conflict,
             Not a iota of grace will be found to take wind.

Positive: Proceed then most hallowed priests with the
             rituals,
             Rest assured, our vigilance shall exceed Argus.

While they poised for the foray, the giant's bellowing din abruptly stopped, throwing the raiders into a quandary. But mustering their confidence, Ambition and Discipline entered the shrine while the two took up positions outside.

As they made towards that Lucifer's statue, a blood curdling howling shrieked, shattering the hush followed by thunder and lightning, an obvious harbinger of the demonic response to the daring challenge. Ambition and Discipline at once halted to look around charily.

Suddenly, out of the forest maze emerged that horrible demon. What a scalding tryst it was! Ambition stood stunned but the rest displayed fortitude.

The hirsute dissembled body vibrating in senescent fits stood gazing in a dour Minotaur's look, as its minatory growling embroiled with vicious hisses spurted out intermittently in the stifling rage.

In my dream, I beheld in a frisson of horror as it advertised disgustingly in a putrid aura and unbearable furrowed countenance drenched with slime; with reddish eyes nestled in the frontal chasm, a craggy nose jutting out, a flame curved jagged ears and a snarling wolves mouth with protracted fangs which was frothing in its forward ferocity.

Before the breaking of hell's flood gate, Lucifer himself leapt from his abominable throne to join the fray; for another petrifying manifestation sparked off inside the shrine; the inert statue began grinning and then let loosed a nerve shattering howl and jerked itself to life!

After this, four semi-limpid spirit beings popped out of the animated statue each clenching a club.

The five iniquitous horrors then with the animate statue clenching a trident made towards the men.

On perceiving that they might be vulnerable, Ambition and Discipline languidly retreated to the shrine's façade.

Meanwhile Positive and Auto rivened, with the former deciding to handle the demon and the latter going to the duo's aid.

Maneuvering adroitly the men soon formed triad battling juggernauts with Positive poised to tackle the demon, Auto confronting the four spirits and the hero and Discipline engaging the animated colossus.

And snapped the hitched chains, with the natural elements of rainstorm, thunder and lightning also joining the horrible encounter!
The demon blasted off in the simulacrum of a thundering Thor or an amok projectile pouncing on Sir Positive, who in a mordant hollering intended to fuel its rage greeted its club with his sword, plunging right into a vortex of an explosive duel.

Simultaneously in a spectacular clash at the abominable façade, the indisputable iron-reed took upon himself a volley of blows from the spooky phalanx, fell back hitting his head against the base of a column, but in no time mustered himself up by giving a frontal thrust with legs, shield and sword, bouncing back to his feet.

While the animated colossus thwarting their strikes with its trident rammed the duo against a shaft which sends Ambition tumbling down the façade stair.

But Discipline infused with the aplomb of a veteran, effervescing fresh courage sprang up to lay upon the hideous horror pounding blows while Ambition refaced to join the battle.

The catastrophic tempest began soaring its intensity as fortune frowned upon the heroic raiders. The high sea-waves were infringing the battle ground to knee-height but as yet to perturb the rage intoxicated combatants.

Now, Sir Positive began falling under the bellowing demon's hammerings while Auto staggeringly defended bravely the shrieking phalanx's gain of an upper hand.

But to my utter grief and shock in my dream, I saw the animated horror ramming Sir Discipline once again against of shaft, who fell down dazzled.

Turning next towards Ambition charged heavily, goring him against a shaft with its horns. Ambition's armour shattered as blood gushed out from his sides and he fell dead pale, groaning.

The revived Discipline then seeing this at once rushed and began battering its back, shifting the horror's focus.

Auto seeing this cried out to Positive for a moment's reprieve so as to aid his master.

As the duel locked Positive, moved down to engage the phalanx, Auto ran to Ambition's aid, helping him up to his feet.

But the argonaut was fatally wounded and could no longer reface to battle.

Had it not been for his armour, Ambition would have been surely instantly killed.

But nonetheless he held on to a nearby tree, biding Auto to resume the conflict.

Now, the horrendous storm grew worse; the flood level rising, currents intensifying and the hellish winds threatening to up-root trees.

The thunders were bellowing, the bolting lightnings were shrieking, and the explosive battle was roaring to ear splitting fury.

But far more than this physical turmoil was now Ambition's inner agonies, as he felt his ebbing life.

But nevertheless, Ambition fought bravely; his screams, yells and stentorian shouts vied with the fiercest thunder itself;

Ambition: Scelptred Aeolus! Halt this storm I say!
Nay, Nay Nay!
Not to thee from the illusive fable of old!
Project O mine voice! Project hence!
Mount upon the winged courser and arise!
Beyond the turgid realm of Hypnos!
To the one who is sitteth by the Righthand!
Yea, thee, do I invoke!
O Aeolus of Tiberius!
Tell me O tell me! what be mine erring!
What be mine follies!
Burning black oxen sacrifice,
By Thrace cavern, to array thine untamed issue
against me-a mortal man of clay!!
Why, why, why!
Why O Patrician of tempest!
Wherefore hast Thou delivered me cruelly,
To the one who once ov'rthrew
The Persian fleet off Cape Sepias!

Meanwhile, clanking of swords and shield, raging bellows, screams, yells and groans of the battling combatants embroiled with rattling strident of leashing thunderstorm like fiery combustion smoke, mushroomed from the singed battle ground.

On the battle front; Sir Positive, in the valour of a blazing comet, indignant fury pouring like devastating lava, fought like a ferocious lion, pounding the demon with volcanic blasting and lightning strikes.

Auto, in battle-trance, possessed with a legion spirits of Bellona and Mars swung his sword like a whirling tornado, blitzing like a spinning rocket in mind shattering insanity—hail storming the phalanx while Discipline in the buzzing of a hornet was warping his stinging strikes upon the animated statue which notwithstanding his paroxysm of hacking obtrudes fell back a little venting gaudy bellows to recoup the set back.

Though in the heat of the battle, Sir Positive was perceptible of Ambition's macabre inner conflict. Calling for Auto, he forthwith disencumbered, rushed towards Ambition:

Ambition: Save me from this opprobrious indigence!
              Remove mine obloquy!
              Nay, Thou would'st not hear!

Positive: Master! Hold thine fort!
              Betray not thine precious donjon!
              Remember, victory is fated in perseverance!
              I can hear the sound of abundance!
              Pepper this fated victory with cheer!
              Hold I say! Sink not the potent rod.
              Hold, hold, hold!

Ambition: But how long! Nay! Mine life ebbs!
              Leave me alone to cross Styx!
              Unstop thine ears, O deaf heavens!
              Loosen thine tongue O Omnipotent King!
              Is thine pacts mere dews!
              Teach not the art to a drowning man!
              Nor the follies of negligence to an injured man!
              Sent not hopes thro' ivory doors!
              Hear me I say! O hear me!
              Thwart this strangling hand of Poverty!
              A broken-reed indeed art thou O heavens!

Positive: Halt thine diving incriminations O master!
              Wreck not this sole salvation plank in this wreck
              itself!

Ambition: Nay, nay nay! I'll vent till I cross Styx anon!
              I will nev'r kiss this divine rod!
              'Tis done! No longer will I kiss!
              Hear me now O unchanging king!
              I behold now my hope in sweet Death!

I invite thee O murderous dagger of Death!
Pierce thine paregoric bodkin and relieve
This forsakened cipher! (Tries to stab himself but
Positive interposes)

Positive: Lay I say! Lay it!
Wreck not the barque at this momentus hour!
Put to sword the Siren's song!
Their faces are fair now!
But aft Styx it turneth fiendish!

Ambition: Wreck thine furies ye thunders!
Here I stand the most worthy target!
A cipher! Heav'n abandoned, cursed wretch!
Wherefore pause! Blast thine bolting cannons!
And consume this wretched casualty!

Positive: Master! Hear me! Avaunt thine ears!
Avaunt thine ears I say!
From the cankerous songs!

Ambition: Nay! How could I!
I now ply past Orkney!
And I can hear that dread voice,
Of Old Man Hoy!
In stygian echoes the voice pursues!
Nor could I break pass Aesma's will!
He's bent on destroying me!
Lo the dry bones hath their hope!
And the Diaspora in the budding of the fig tree!
But what hope hast this dry bones!
Mine ignominy and imbroglios, yea dire woes!
Hath wax a woeful Aeneid!
All to the delight of scornful society!

Positive: Would'st thou not permit the Orpheus of Hope!
To out-play the enchanting songs!
Seal thine ears! Anon we'll steer pass our Argo!

Ambition: Mine night hast come! Here I stand!
              Upon the eleventh hour!
              Behold the Summanusian thunderbolts! Tis sore
              wroth!
              The immortal wounds hast even defied Dr. Time!
              Prithee leave me alone to cross Styx!

Discipline: Avast I say! Such stoical acquiescence!
              Behold O argonaut! Behold I say! Behold now!
              Thou stand'st upon the sacret Alatuir!
              The streams of hope, floweth neath thine very feet!
              Be of good cheer I say!
              Deliverance is at hand! Swoon not in thine vigil!
              Anon thou shalt see him thine deliverer—the
              invincible man, Mr. Other-Self!
              Would'st thou see thine enemies prosper,
              And defile thine name! Nay!
              Wilt thou not permit Other-Self to dilt thine arch
              adversary, Unemployment!
              Wilt thou die O coward, before beholding,
              The terrible powers of the invincible man!
              Would'st thou die!! Speak out O argonaut!
              Wilt thou die before seeing the carnage,
              Wreaked upon thine enemies!
              By thine redeemer, Mr. Other-Self!
              Would'st thou die now! Tell me O argonaut!

Ambition: Nay, nay, nay! I would not die!

Positive: Look yond! Thy men battling!
              Drench in blood, bath in wounds!
              All for thine life O master art we laying ours!
              Would'st thou die now! But nay, regard us not!
              Think again of thine Other-Self, who shalt anon
              come unto thine aid!

Ambition: Nay, nay, nay! Let me not die without seeing him,
              Mine great deliverer! Nor am I alone!
              O mine alter ego, thee and him Mr. Other-Self!

And all mine alter egos are now waxed,
An Amazon Girdle! Let's now arise!
The siren's vapours are passed! Hasten O Positive,
unto Auto's aid!

Now back to the hubbub battle field: Discipline and the animate stature were in frizzling embrace; grappling each other in a horrid huff, were wrestling violently; ducking each other's head forcefully into the waist height waters.

Auto, engaging the five, that is the demon and the four spooky horrors, had dragged the battle up to a nearby hill, free from the flood.

The fiery Auto, beefed up with such indefatigable might, outmatching Antaeus himself rumbled forth in the bloody hullabaloo like a bristling battling juggernaut; hacking with sword, thwarting with shield, pounding with kicks, shouts of rambunctious yells, cutting, thrusting, hammering, piercing his way to the very gates of hell!

Sir Positive, wading through the waters, up-reared and pounced upon the hellish group with ear shattering yells; he took upon the spooky phalanx for a change, while Auto locked up with the demon.

Positive, confident of the cinch now began maneuvering wittily until he broke up the phalanx and soon the spooks fell one by one to his sword.

Meanwhile Sir Discipline was still in the reek of the duel with the animated colossus. Victorious Positive

now ran to Auto's aid and together they battered and mauled the demon to death.

After this the duo immediately charged towards the waters to join Discipline.

The three of them then began strafing the animated colossus, desiccating its powers till it collapsed in pieces.

What a victory it was!
In the éclat, they joyfully razed the entire temple to rubble thus uprooting the evil sojourn to the delight and joy of Ambition.

After this they nursed their wounds especially the dying argonaut with strange herbs and then headed towards the mountain valley to meet the giant, Sub-Conscious.

Auto: A peaen to our banner!
     'Sing Victory! Sing Victory!
     For the battle is to our unconquerable souls,
     T'will nev'r crawl neath the yoke,
     But t'will take thee, O Evil,
     By thine horns!'

Ambition: Galant Auto, thine peaen promulgating the glorious
     anathema a while ago of the evil sojourn,
     Doth ring melodies Unto mine ears!
     Tho' the Pygmalion shock, did strike me like a sea-
     anemone's tentacle,
     And did away with mine fortitude,
     Yet, the presence of ye, worked upon me wondrously
     like the hoisted potent rod.
     O the devotion and the love fetters,
     Which bind ye to me even surpasses the Damonian
     faithfulness.
     Truth I say unto ye;
     Pythias shall surely envy me,
     For he hath but one alter ego, but I three.

Discipline: Beguiled by her brightness, thou forget'st
     That there are other graces than Aglaia.
     Hark, there await thine other servitors
     Back in the Kingdom who in truth deserve
     The equal shares of thine fruit. Hearken then;

<blockquote>
For this purpose we exist, 'Tis to lay
Our lives at thine behest, to be counted
As sheep ready for slaughter and to shield
Thee from thine enemies' arrows.
</blockquote>

Ambition: O mine dear alter egos, finding such
      Solicitude and source is as seeking
      The will-O-the-wisp Other-Self himself.
      Harken; how strange a world me-seems. But thus
      The round unvarnished tale of wight's kingdom;
      Men are indeed alien to one another.

Positive: I canst not perceive!

Ambition: Incline then thyself to a quintessence;
      The celestial Canopus that glitters,
      The earthly Pyxie that creeps and deep's star
      Which gracefully glides, though akin in name
      And shape, yet are alien to one another.
      Thus like manner are the homo sapians;
      For with strange motleys are their carriages
      Composed; selfish misanthropes whose evil,
      Purposed heart knoweth but for to envy
      Hate, look upon with contempt and belittle
      His neighbours, Hubris glozed, lofty-headed
      Miscreants in elevated positions, whose
      Depraved nature delights upon oppressing
      The poor and the weak and whose evil delight
      Sharpens when vassals in their false allegiance
      And obsequious submissions doth pander
      To their self-conceit. The sea when waxing
      Tempest we behold the wroth of its
      Rip-tide, but when it ceases, the neap-tide
      Blazons its gentleness. For yet there are
      The meek and the lowly, the philanthropists
      Who despite the evil clime of a selfish
      World, are moved with such compassion, pity
      For their neighbours though 'Tis, but a sight rare.

Wherefore such gulfs among men, I know not.
But truly no greater wealth or riches
Can a man find than alter egos like ye
And the fabulous GreatWithin.

Discipline: If we wert to reckon Pyrrho's conceit,
For me-seems there doth lie some great elements
Of truth when he contended that all knowledge
Is but broken-reed, the homo-sapian's
Foundation is uncertain and should nev'r
Be taken as a fount of aid or help.
For selfishness doth persist in the good
And the bad; so vouches the saying which says-
Can a libbard, yea both the ferocious
And the tame change its spot? Nay, it cannot!
But the Ancient of Days hath so purposed
By His infinite wisdom when He laid
The foundation of our existence that
Perforce some elements remain eternal
And immutable and reliable, of which
GreatWithin and thine alter egos are.

They at last reached the valley and immediately met the sane giant; who had a stalwart physique perhaps like Hercules. The giant then accosted them:

Sub-Conscious: Greetings noble men—what cheer! Whence came ye?

Discipline: Good, dear giant! From GreatWithin are we come.

Sub-Conscious: 'Tis mine bounden duty to entertain
Your boons. But must I needs to make amend
For some strength and pow'rs I lost by reason
Of a strange incubus which hath vexed me
But left a while ago. I know not what waxed
Of me. Me-seens I did possess lately

A beastly carriage. But nevertheless,
What's your purpose?

Positive: We've come to present thee with Grendel's head!
Rejoice evermore mighty giant, we've avenged
Thine vexation and cruel bondage.

Sub-Cons: My Beowulfs! T'was ye who turned mine captivity!
Blest be the work! I know not how to thank,
T'will nev'r go unreaped. Hark, at your behest,
This servitor is ready to scale up
The highest mount, or dive neath the deep
Or crush titans and kingdoms! Boons make known!

Discipline: Hearken then thou giant, to thine master!

Ambition: I am come to seek that mysterious man,
The invincinble Mr. Other-Self . . .

Sub-Cons: Nay, nay, nay! Not him my good master!
Gladly will I battle mega titans
Than to seek that terrible Other-Self!
O I plead! O I beg! Please slay me not
With this task. Look! it is not proper for you,
To send to feeble lamb to a great lion!

Ambition: If thus the strong tower I find in thee
Then hark, I will no longer strive with you
In this matter. But there is another boon
I would ask of thee. Wilt thou grant!

Sub-Cons: Heartily O master. Just make known.

Ambition: O titan and mine dear Alter Egos,
Prithee, grant yours ears and hearts to mine song;
Titan! Behold the wounds immortal,
As life ebbs from mine portal
Wherefore doth this destitute man pleads?

Wrecked brutally by Unemployment's deeds.
Garden of Sorrow waxed mine insurmountable
mount,
But spurned that everlasting fount.
Then, a healing stream by Bouyan I did learn
Of its splendour and hope I sore yearn,
But refuseth that sacred Alatuir to open neath;
Mine dream, mine cornucopia I'll n'ver meet.
Titan! Alas mine effigy; thou hast failed me,
My Hope! My Life! Will I ever see?
O, will-O-the-wisp Other-Self,
Dost thou any compassion or solicitude have?
Even upon thine immortal slumber,
Dreamed thou of this destitude ever?
Lo, cometh she with her shear grin
Night Clotho's thread that's now is spin
Save me O mysterious man!
For mine hour of ignomious doom is at hand!
Arise from thine slumbering throne,
Lift me from the raging maelstrom of Acheron,
Make haste O Other-Self, make haste!
That I may n'ver of bitter scorn taste
Upon this labyrinth what shall be mine contend
For the waxing of the v'r lasting fount
Lorn? Haply I dwell in the age of iron!
Therefore mine only! Only hope art thou
O mysterious man!

With this Ambition dies! With the shocking death
Auto found himself in limbo.

Auto: Brutal Destiny! Set thou the requilm
For twain! Gone art thou, O dear Pyramus,
Arcadian swain, leaving behind thine lass-
Grief smitten Thisbe! What be thine purpose,
Joy or hope hereafter? O my master,
The veil of Styx—it will no longer be

A bulwark betwixt us. Here I cross! (stabs himself
and dies)

Discipline: Brutal Time! Wherefore hast thou treacherously
Betrayed my master to Hades?
Thine sore tantalized yearn,
Bled to death upon a barren land,
Relentlessly spurned by Hope's hand
Titan! Of thine stubbornness will thou not turn?'
Alas! if by death I could this craggy heart
Move, then, embrace I thee O death! O death!

(stabs himself and dies)

Positive: Fie! fie on me! stood I helpless and weak
When that rotten Shear-Wielder made amain
To wrest sway of thine barque, O argonaut!
Hath I but hastened unto thine sore want
At the Garden, thou would'st have scaped those
wounds!
Wherefore such shadow of turnings O Fates;
Engendering mine delay thence, Time to bribe
Its way to possess Elijah's feet, while me
To abode the swift chariot. O alas!
But nay! Let our deaths be immortal seeds.
The positive seeds to good thee titan!
Here I throw (kills himself)

Chapter 13

The Great Awakening of Mr. Other-Self

Sub-Cons: O Shock! Dost thou possess any season!
O Positive Emotion!
Thy seething word thaws the coldness of mine heart.
O argonaut, hadst thou not been embarrassed by myopia,
Thou would'st have surely vanquished mine great heart,
And reached the strond of hope.
O Ambition,
Hast thou taken upon thyself the quietus of the seven sleepers of Ephesus;
Reposing thine bitterness in the springs of Lethe!
Alas! thine life hath taken wings to a land far, far beyond;
As far as the Austral Crucifix is from Delphinus by north.
Cruel Hades!
Hadst thou absconded with thine catch so quickly across Styx!
Ah! Verily shall thine will, purpose, prosper as of that smart Centauraus by Evenus!
Take heed O Hades!
Thou wilt anon taste the deadly arrow of the mysterious man—the invincible Mr. Other-Self!
Fear not O argonaut!

The mysterious man, shalt anon hasten unto thine rescue!
And thou shalt behold the lightning splendours,
Of that Grene Gome upon great grene steed!
Harken now O mysterious man, Other-Self!
Mine boundless wisdom outplays thy mysteries!
Who art thou? Yea, that I know!
What art thou? Yea, I know!
Where art thou? Yea, I know!
'Tis in the far, far beyond—the seventh Cosmic dimension,
Of which I and I alone can penetrate!
Neath that bottomless mount sleep'st thou O sleeping giant!

The giant then stooped to search the dead argonaut's bossom and took out that garnet stone and then continued solemnly:

Sub-Cons: For reason is confounded, wisdom appalled,
O strange stone! In thee is lurked those powers,
So mysterious, to awaken that sleeping giant!
Yea the instant thou O stone touch'st that mysterious man!
By gad! That terrible, yea horrendous, yea hideous awakening shall begin!
Gad! what awakening t'will be!
Even to wean of it, I swoon for fear;
That mount shall belch out fiery molten rocks,
Burst, crumble, hurling raging fragments for and wide,
O how the entire dimension, shall be shaken to its very foundation!
O how the earth shall rent apart, tremor!
By gad! Haply I may be even killed In this hideous awakening! O my God!
Where shall I then seek refuge after casting This garnet stone down the mountain's chasm?
By some distant mounts?

Even then t'will be like seeking canopy by a toad-
stool!
For even this island and GreatWithin shall shake with
the mighty reverberation of the great catastrophic
awakening of that mysterious man, invincible giant,
Sir Other-Self!
By gad! What awakening!
Poverty!
Wherefore such frills and furbelows, about thine
despotic powers?
Take heed! Ye hosts of evil!
For out of the seventh Cosmic Dimension,
Yea there shall arise A Man!
Yea that storied giant! His name—the invincible
giant, Sir Other-Self!
Lo and behold all ye titanic hosts;
For he Sir Other-Self shall arise to visit ye with the
punitive rewards!
Nay, the come-uppance!
This Sir Other-Self:
He shall rip apart the dread lower world;
Keeping his tryst there without an obolus,
But shall give Charon instead, a tight slap on his
cheek,
Bind him hand and foot and thence,
Ferry him down the dark meandering Styx.
In promethean vault next,
Landing upon the liquidified fires of Phlegethon,
He'll tame the snake-locked Furies with vengeance,
After which shall thrashed Allecto,
With loud wailings fall prostrate in repentance to
kiss the feet of Aeneas begging his pardon.
He shall thence divert the gloomy courses of
Archeron and Cocytus thro' Elysian Realms,
Squirting the doleful waters into the mouths of the
feasting Homeric gods,
To swirl out their scornful laughter;
There aft shall they eternally weep sorrowfully.

Nor shall he fail to visit Pluto's throne;
Upon entrance gate shall Sir Other-Self,
Brush aside with a fatal kick the hound, Cerberus,
Which would flee howling in pain with blushing
tail hid betwixt its hind legs.
Petrified Medusa upon seeing his gaze,
Shall herself be turned to inanimate stone.
Grapping then trembling Pluto by his neck,
Shall hurl him down the deep of Tartarus.
Nor shall those three withered old Fates escape;
The spinning-jenny will he hoist and say:
"Clotho! Here, take this!" Dash't against her head,
Hustling down next Larchersis by her hair,
Shall he with one kick send her rolling on her own
threads;
Snatching away the abhorred shear,
Shall he then shave off bald, helpless long tress
Atropos;
Thus will the Fates go, riding on donkeys in
sackcloth and ash to mourn their own fate.
Then shall Morpheus have his gloomy nightmares.
These are but a tenth of the dread mayhem,
He the mysterious giant—Sir Other-Self,
Shall wreak upon Lord Poverty's Kingdom.
I must now make haste!

With this the giant lifted his right arm and suddenly a whirlwind
swooped and ravished him off at a lightning speed. Beholding
the four dead man in my dream, especially the protonogist, the
argonaut and former destitute man from Penury, Sir Ambition, did
throw me on to some profound reminiscent of the saga.

Yet to set out on his odyssey, and being storm-bound at the garden
of sorrow, he found it a horrid labyrinth at the same time hope
was so tantalizing, always falling short of fruition even with the
serendipity of the GreatWithin and the alter egos. The pathos
moved my heart to tears.

But above all the metaphysical confusion centered upon the mysteries of the invincible man was both appalling and intriguing as there were no ground to procure or decipher any definite conclusion from the giant's paradoxical alluding; who generally refers him as a man, sometimes as a giant while other times a knight.

Now, can these four men, especially the hero Sir Ambition receive hope, in fact supernatural hope! Well, what if . . . I hear something! Can it be! It's getting louder now! My friends I think this must be it! Oh No! The island now tremors! Rocks and boulders come rumbling down now all over this place! I hear now the mountains exploding afar a far off! Yes I can even faintly see far off at a distant land a fiery belch of fuming flames!

By gad! This must be the awakening of that strange mysterious man, Sir Other-Self! Yes my friends, he has awakened! The mysterious man, Other-Self has awakened! Nothing is going to be impossible now!

There is going to be hope for the dead Sir Ambition and all the dead heroic gladiators with this awakening of the invincible giant, Sir Other-Self!

And I woke from my sleep. And behold, it was just a dream!

(To be continued in part II)

OTHER PAPERBACK PRINTED BOOKS
BY B MATHEW

I AM THE ALPHA & OMEGA

Published in Malaysia thro' The Inspiration Hub: paperback book for Malaysian Christian bookstores. Perpustakaan Negara Malaysia Cataloguing-in-Publication Data: Mathew, B., 1957-I am the alpha & omega / B. Mathew.—2nd Ed. ISBN 978-967-10340-0-2 1. Christian life-- Biblical teaching. 2. Christianity--Prayers and devotions

This book is AVAILABLE at:

1.   Perpustakaan Negara Malaysia, KL & Malaysia's National Book Collection Centres in Sg Besi, KL, Penang & Sabah

2.   PNB Online Public Access Catalogue (OPAC)

The Inspiration Hub—http://www.theinspirationhub.com/b-mathew/i-am-the-alpha-omega

Amazon Digital Services—http://www.amazon.com/dp/B005DKY6RA

3.   Salvation Book Centre branches & Glad Sounds book store branches (Klang Valley Only)

4.   Canaanland book stores

5.   Ebenezer Bookland, KL

6.   The Attributes (City Harvest Church bookstore), PJ

RESTORATION OF BROKEN-RELATIONSHIPS,

SEPARATIONS & DIVORCES

PUBLISHED IN USA BY

RED LEAD PRESS

PITTSBURGH, PENNSYLVANIA

Copyright © 2011 by B MATHEW

ISBN: 1-4349-6664-3

DO YOU WANT HEALING FOR YOUR BROKEN-RELATIONSHIPS & MARITAL BREAKDOWNS?

In this book, the author says, as you <u>WALK OUT OF YOUR ROOM IN TORN CLOTH, SHRIVELED HAIR, and IN MUD, SLIME, BLACK-EYES AND BRUISES ALL OVER YOU,</u> your BROKEN-RELATIONSHIP, SEPARATION AND DIVORCE WILL BE RESTORED & HEALED BY A MIRACLE OF RECONCILIATION.

The author addresses today's social disease of marital divorces and separation. Whether you are estranged from your spouse or from your loved ones, your family, your friends, your children, your parents, your church members, your pastors, your business partners & associates or from any one, the author avers the eternal truth that THERE'S NO BROKEN RELATIONSHIP WHICH CHRIST CANNOT HEAL.

The author speaks about root causes of present day divorces amongst Christians;
* Affliction of generational curses or spiritual affliction

* One's own inner attitude and mind frame

* Personality traits in individuals

* Direct attacks & causes by demons

And how to tear down these root causes and bring about miracles of restoration for any kind of broken relationships.

The Parable of the Prodigal Son in Luke 15:11-31, tells you how the younger son became estranged and suffered a broken relationship with not only his loved ones, but his own relationship with God the Father was also broken down. But the prodigal son, stopped blaming the devil, others and God, and came to his senses. And thereafter, a miracle of reconciliation took place in his life and there came a HAPPY ENDING in his life. A HAPPY ENDING WAITS FOR YOU TOO.

As you read the messages, you too can grasp the revelation of <u>WALKING OUT OF YOUR ROOM IN TORN CLOTH, SHRIVELED HAIR, and IN MUD, SLIME, BLACK-EYES AND BRUISES ALL OVER YOU</u> for the healing of your nightmares of broken-relationships, separation and divorce.

MESSAGES OF FAITH & DELIVERANCE

These short messages by B Mathew, is a concise version of his sermons preached behind pulpits and evangelistic meetings since the 1970's.

These are fundamental gospel faith messages delivered under the anointing of the Holy Spirit.

The power of God's Word will break, shatter every bondage and yoke tormenting you as you read through these messages and appropriate the prayers at the end.

Therefore, you are advised to first prepare your heart, remove all distractions before reading these messages. You can expect the miracle power of Christ to surge through you while reading these messages.

The author wants all readers to experience a direct encounter with the power of Christ thro' these messages.

As you read these messages, fears, depression, all unbelief and every tormenting thoughts will be driven out of you and new faith, fresh boldness and a renewed mind will come into your life. And you will see miracles, healings and deliverance flow easily into your life because of this new found faith.

GOD'S GIFT OF ETERNAL LIFE

This rich man in the parable cared a lot about his material life, his social standing and about his appearance, bought the finest clothes, drove the latest cars, lived in the finest house, was member of the finest club in town, was the finest RELIGIOUS man in town.

But he forgot that going deeper down his outer temporary body, he was actually a living SOUL, the real him who needed the **gift of eternal life** which Jesus offers.

The rich man in the parable neglected his Soul and as a result he found himself in Hell fires.

Are you neglecting your Soul today?

When you receive this Gift of Eternal Life from Jesus Christ after your sins are forgiven, you can be assured that when you die and leave your earthly life, your soul would be received up to Heaven where you will spend your eternity with Christ.

But if your sins are not cleansed by the blood of Jesus, your soul will perish in eternal death in Hell fires where your soul would be tormented for eternity.

But God has paid a terrible price for YOU! God crucified His only begotten Son, Jesus on the Cross for YOU.

So that, if you come to Christ in repentance, your sins will be forgiven and thereafter you will receive the Gift of Eternal Life.

THE SPIRIT OF PROPHECY—(The

God who speaks through Dreams

& Visions)

- Does God speak to people today? The primary means He speaks today is thro' His written Word, the Bible.

- But God also uses a secondary means to speak to you today. And that is, via dreams & visions.

- In this prophetic writing, you will be forced to rethink currently practiced norms, gimmicks and teachings of the materialistic church of today.

- You will learn God's strategies in dealing with coming natural disasters, escalation of crime rates, destruction of marriages, child murders, Extremism, Church splits / crises and others.

- No longer will you stand helpless.

- You will be shown an insight into the spirit world to understand how a prophet of God operates via dreams and visions.

- The author reveals a hidden and mysterious concept buried deep inside the Biblical principle of Tithing, which the present day church has failed to discover.

- Lastly, how to receive and operate in the supernatural prophetic gifting.

b mathew's Tag Cloud:

alpha omega   angelic help   **bmathew**   brokenrelationships
career   career change   deliverance   dismissal   divorces   dreams   east
window   emotional healing   employment   faith   healing   inspirational
john bunyan   john milton   jurisprudence   law   legal   legends   literature
livelihood   myths   overcomer   paradise lost   philosophy   pilgrims progress
poetry   prayer victories   prophecies   repentance   revival   salvation
separations   skills   talents   visions

SMASHWORDS ebook TITLES by B Mathew

Ambition's Progress Part 1

Ebook USD. 36250 words. Fiction by b mathew *on August 17, 2011*
ISBN: 978-1-4661-2285-7

An allegory written by B Mathew. Written in flowery classical English of prose and verse. It has abundant allusions, bringing to life and excitement the beauty of classical mythology, western legends, Biblical stories, literature and poetry. This archaic writing of an allegory set in poetical verses may not fit contemporary literature.

Breaking Strongholds Thro' Mid-Night Prayers

Ebook Price: $0.99 USD. 2350 words. Non-Fiction by b mathew *on August 19, 2011*
ISBN: 978-1-4659-5327-8

Are you struggling in your prayer iife without breakthroughs & results? Learn what is a Mid-Night Experience & why it brings about spectacular results & breakthroughs. Your prayer life will never be the same again. A short Message by B Mathew

Are You Neglecting Your Soul Today

Ebook Price: $0.99 USD. 6250 words. Non-Fiction by b mathew *on August 19, 2011*
ISBN: 978-1-4660-7992-2.

Are you on the road to Hell Fires? 3 fundamental Gospel Messages of repentance by B Mathew

Learn to Release Warrior Angels Into your Life's Problems

Ebook Price: $0.99 USD. 2380 words. Non-Fiction by b mathew *on August 19, 2011*
ISBN: 978-1-4661-8464-0.

A short message by B Mathew. Are you struggling in desperation today? Your life in total mess, without hope? Unemployment, business failure, debts,troubles?

Cheer-up! The God of the Bible will send His mighty warrior angels to deliver you. Learn to release the power of warrior angels.

God Can Transform Your Career Life today

Ebook Price: $0.99 USD. 4850 words. Non-Fiction by b mathew *on August 21, 2011*

ISBN: 978-1-4659-8304-6

Another life changing short Message by B Mathew. Are you stuck in a job where you are frustrated, redundant, boring, without progress? Make a 180 degrees change by leting Christ touch & anointing those hidden skills within you. And then see what happens next.

EAST WINDOWS OF LIFE

Ebook Price: $0.99 USD. 13060 words. Non-Fiction by b mathew *on August 16, 2011*

ISBN: 978-1-4660-8550-3

Disappointments & Job-frustrations? Fulfillment & Breakthroughs await in the EAST WINDOW of your life Move away from the WEST WINDOWS—That's where you rot & decay.

Restoration of Broken-Relationships, Separations & Divorces

Ebook Price: $0.99 USD. 23830 words. Non-Fiction by b mathew *on August 16, 2011*

ISBN: 978-1-4659-0779-0

RESTORATION OF BROKEN-RELATIONSHIPS, SEPARATIONS & DIVORCES DO YOU WANT HEALING FOR YOUR BROKEN-RELATIONSHIP & MARITAL BREAKDOWN? In this book, the author says, as you WALK OUT OF YOUR ROOM IN TORN-CLOTH, SHRIVELED HAIR, and IN MUD, SLIME, BLACK-EYES AND BRUISES ALL OVER YOU, your BROKEN-RELATIONSHIP, SEPARATION AND DIVORCE WILL BE RESTORED.

RIVERS OF THE HOLY GHOST

Ebook Price: $0.99 USD. 2010 words. Non-Fiction by b mathew *on August 19, 2011*

ISBN: 978-1-4661-5062-1

RIVERS OF THE HOLY GHOST

BREAKING MISFORTUNES & BAD-LUCKS IN YOUR LIFE

Ebook Price: $0.99 USD. 1990 words. Non-Fiction by b mathew *on*
August 19, 2011
ISBN: 978-1-4658-3470
BREAKING MISFORTUNES & BAD-LUCKS IN YOUR LIFE

The God Who Heals All Unpardonable Mistakes

Ebook Price: $0.99 USD. 1970 words. Non-Fiction by b mathew *on*
August 21, 2011
ISBN: 978-1-4657-0340-8
Have you committed an unpardonable mistake in life? Let Christ heal you today.
A short Message by B Mathew

Changing Your Disgrace & Shame Into Honour

Ebook Price: $0.99 USD. 5480 words. Non-Fiction by b mathew *on*
August 21, 2011
ISBN: 978-1-4661-6568-7
Has the Stars, Fate and Fortune condemned you to a life of disgrace, failure
& misfortune. I have Good News for YOU. The Living Christ can turn your
disgrace into Honour today.

The Spirit of Prophecy pt 1

Ebook Price: $0.99 USD. 8630 words. Non-Fiction by b mathew *on*
August 22, 2011
ISBN: 978-1-4658-5550-3
THE GOD WHO SPEAKS THRO' DREAMS & VISIONS

The Spirit of Prophecy pt 2

Ebook Price: $0.99 USD. 22870 words. Non-Fiction by b mathew *on*
August 22, 2011
ISBN: 978-1-4657-0186-2.
The God who speaks thro' dreams & visions

BE SET FREE—Sinful Addictions, Sickness & Misfortunes

Ebook Price: $0.99 USD. 4520 words. Non-Fiction by b mathew *on*
September 4, 2011
ISBN: 978-1-4660-7381-4.
3 Powerful Deliverance Messages by B Mathew

I AM THE ALPHA & OMEGA

Ebook Price: $0.99 USD. 6950 words. Non-Fiction by b mathew *on*
August 14, 2011
ISBN: 978-1-4661-5528-2.
Have you felt forsaken by God? Have you felt overwhelmed by Satan? Have you felt your prayers go unanswered? John in Patmos felt the same. But Jesus appeared to John with 3 great revelations. John's life totally transformed and he went on to write the greatest book in the New Testament. Your life too will never be the same again as Jesus comes to you, touches you through the life-changing . . .

Author Pages

Amazon's Complete Selection of B Mathew Books

Discover books, read about the author, find related products, and more. **Read more at Amazon's B Mathew Page**
Bestselling Books: I AM THE ALPHA & OMEGA.

AMAZON KINDLE ebook TITLES by B Mathew

1.

I AM THE ALPHA & OMEGA by b mathew (Kindle Edition—19 Jul 2011)—Kindle eBook
Buy: £0.86. Available for download now

2.

GIFT OF ETERNAL LIFE by B MATHEW (Kindle Edition—1 Aug 2011)—Kindle eBook
Buy: £0.86. Available for download now

3.

RESTORATION OF BROKEN-RELATIONS, SEPARATIONS & DIVORCES by B MATHEW (Kindle Edition—3 Aug 2011)—Kindle eBook
Buy: £0.86. Available for download now

4.

Fulfillment & Breakthroughs AWAIT IN THE EAST WINDOWS by B MATHEW (Kindle Edition—3 Aug 2011)—Kindle eBook
Buy: £0.86 Available for download now

5.

The Greatest Prophet in the Bible by B Mathew (Kindle Edition—18 Aug 2011)—Kindle eBook
Buy: £0.86. Available for download now

6.

The Prodigal Son by B Mathew (Kindle Edition—18 Aug 2011)—Kindle eBook
Buy: £0.86 Available for download now

7.

I Believe in Angels by B Mathew (Kindle Edition—18 Aug 2011)—Kindle eBook
<u>Buy</u>: £0.86 Available for download now

8.

The Easter Message by B Mathew (Kindle Edition—18 Aug 2011)—Kindle eBook
<u>Buy</u>: £0.86 Available for download now

9.

BREAKING MISFORTUNES & BAD-LUCKS IN YOUR LIFE by B Mathew (Kindle Edition—18 Aug 2011)—Kindle eBook